PUBLIC SERVANT . . . PRIVATE ENEMY

In her experience policemen were large, crude, domineering. Herr Karl-Heinz Staengel was small, wiry, and hard. He came across the thick carpet, holding out his hand and crinkling his ice-blue eyes in a smile that scarcely reached his straight-edged mouth.

"Please believe that I realize how worried you are. It is because of this that I have agreed to see you. But in fact, Fraulein Viner, nothing can be done to find your father at this time."

He dropped his card on the table in front of her. She was dismissed.

The next day she saw his file. Former SS major, former guard at the Sachsdenhausen Concentration Camp, former SS staff during the liquidation of the Hungarian Jews.

Now she knew why he had refused to help her. She also knew why she was being followed. And why suddenly she had to fear for her own life . . .

Berlin Epitaph

Alan Winnington

PINNACLE BOOKS • **NEW YORK CITY**

This is a work of fiction. All the characters and events portrayed in this book are fictional. Any resemblance to real people or incidents is purely coincidental.

BERLIN EPITAPH

Copyright © 1973 by Alan Winnington

A Pinnacle book, formerly titled *Berlin Halt*, published by special arrangement with Robert Hale & Company, London.

ISBN: 0-523-00421-4

First printing, September 1974

Printed in the United States of America

PINNACLE BOOKS, INC.
275 Madison Avenue
New York, N.Y. 10016

CONTENTS

1	Viner	7
2	Shadowed	25
3	Dietrich	43
4	Blue Tattoo	54
5	Kessel's Fingerprints	65
6	Scottish Accent	76
7	Showdown	90
8	West Berlin	97
9	Agent	104
10	Koll's Fingerprints	113
11	Death in Wedding	120
12	Dietrich Surfaces	131
13	End of the Spoor	143
14	Ginglass	154
15	News of Blake	165
16	At Bay	175

ONE

VINER

EACH leaf was still green in the middle. Then came a ring of yellow and a thin edge of brown. One part of Unter den Linden had been newly laid and fallen leaves had been driven into the tarmac turning the wet road into a green-gold-brown carpet. The sky turned pewter, lights came on, people hurried home to *abendbrot*.

A bad day for killing time. Half an hour to wait until rain washed away the rest of the daylight.

It was bright and warm inside the foyer of the Berolina Hotel, packed with people occupying every table. The Mongolian tourists were still there, counting their puzzling change and pointing to what they wanted at the bar. One table was surrounded by carefree Russians, each with a bottle of beer. They had two bottles of vodka in common and were eating salami and salted fish.

A big group of assorted types had just arrived on a sightseeing tour from West Berlin: American soldiers with their wives; a few British in baggy turned-up trousers; a Japanese pair who shared one bottle of cola. Most of the Americans were writing postcards—"Here I am behind the Iron Curtain. . . ." At some unseen signal, the whole group flocked out and piled into a glass topped bus.

East Berlin was done. This evening there would be an all-in tour of the West Berlin night spots.

Suddenly the foyer returned to normal. With sighs of relief the girls started to clear the debris.

The bar had emptied too and there was room to put a leg over a stool. A cognac—just one—and a beer; then into the restaurant for a trout. And then it would be time.

It was a good trout, swimming in browned butter, but he resisted the temptation to order a bottle of white wine. No drinking tonight.

Coffee came and he paid for his meal at the same time.

"Mr. Viner?"

The diner looked up, nodded.

The other waited. The man addressed as Viner remembered his cue.

"Would you care to join me in a double-mocca?"

"Thank you but at present I am forbidden coffee."

"I am sorry to hear that."

Everything was in order.

"I have something for you."

"And I for you."

"Have you settled your bill?"

"Yes."

"Shall we go?"

"The sooner the better, before the crowds thin out."

There were twenty or so people waiting to cross the border at the Friedrichstrasse "glasshouse". He would have preferred more but it would have to do.

In exchange for the passport he got a numbered slip and watched the slim blue book with its oblong patches of white slide through the slot into somewhere where it would be processed. He lit a cigarette and waited. This was where the trouble would come if it came and where he would have to think on his feet. Numbers were called and people went to the counter, moving on after to the customs.

At last the passport slid out of the slot again and he went to the counter before his number was called.

He handed over his numbered slip and the officer compared it with the part he had retained. He took his time. He opened the passport and looked at the photo, back to the man and back again to the photo.

He felt the sweat breaking out but took the cigarette from his mouth to give the officer a better look.

"Mister Viner," the officer said, "I would recommend a better photograph. This is hardly recognizable."

He spoke in German.

"Sorry. My German is not good."

"Photo. *Nicht gut*. Not good," he added in English.

"Ah, yes. Old."

"You have been over before, I see."

"Business."

The magic word.

"Thank you. That is all."

At the next counter he handed over the customs declaration, filled in and signed.

"No presents? Valuables?"

"Nothing."

"Money?"

"Forty-five Westmarks."

"Marks of the German Democratic Republic?"

"None."

"Thank you. That is all, good night."

A Wansee train was waiting in the S-Bahn, empty. The Intershop was closing but he managed to persuade the girl to let him have a bottle of Scotch. He needed a drink.

But he waited. They might still come running up the stairs.

"Wansee train. Get in please. Stand back."

It clattered through the border. There were the outlines of the Reichstag on the left. He unscrewed the patent top and took a long drink of whisky.

Even in Bond Street, men took an extra look at Mary Penny. She had rebuffed quite a few oblique and some direct offers of advancement for certain considerations. But in spite of that, she knew that a lot of her success in newspaper work was due less to her brain than her long legs, almost black hair, great dark eyes and full, stubborn mouth. She was no fool, though, and tall enough to make her presence felt, slim and hard-muscled for coping with the opposition, irresistible to policemen and commissionaires.

Much more important—she could sit down at a typewriter and write at any required length precisely that kind of saccharine "human interest" journalism which non-thinking, scarcely-able-to-read housewives instantly recognised as "exactly what I had thought all along". Into lives between the supermarket and the kitchen sink, Mary Penny brought romance, helped them to feel that they were not so badly off after all, that Money Made People Unhappy, and above all that the true place of woman was in the home and caring for the comfort of her husband. None of which Mary believed.

Mary wrote in this way because she worked for the *Phoenix*—what Fleet Street calls a popular daily, meaning that it is rather a magazine than a newspaper, light reading for the mob.

Mary pressed the buzzer of Steve Blake's flat, waited a moment and pressed it again impatiently.

He came to the door, a cooking spatula in one hand and a shirt tied by its sleeves round his waist as an apron. The entrance was filled with the smell of spices and garlic. Holding the spatula so that it could not drip, he gave her a garlicky kiss.

"Steve," she said excitedly, "you have just kissed Mary Penny, by-lined columnist of the *Phoenix*, with contract."

He clicked his heels and saluted smartly with the hand holding the spatula. A row of oil spots appeared on the wall.

At best he was no more than an inch taller than she, forty-ish and getting plump above the navel and under the chin, which was bluish. His nose was well-chiselled and pointed and set in a muscular face, despite the dawning fat. Under a forehead getting higher with the years, were quick intelligent eyes. Steve was chief crime reporter of the *Daily Success*, main rival of the *Phoenix*.

"How much?" he asked.

"Ten quid a week rise to be reviewed in six months."

"Marvellous," he began and then stopped with a look of horror, sniffing.

"The pepper!"

He flung open the kitchen door, releasing a billow of blue smoke and plunged into it. Mary caught the next wave of smoke and through tear-blurred eyes she saw Steve struggling with one hand to get the window open. Coughing and cursing he thrust the frying pan outside and leaned out. Gradually the air cleared.

Pots and jars littered the table, along with the debris of onions, garlic and cabbage. A casserole was simmering on the stove.

Steve said, "Pour us a drink. I'll have to start that again."

"What is it? Tear gas?"

"Peppered beef and orange. Lovely!"

She shuddered, handed him a glass and then lifted the casserole lid. "What's in here?"

"Common cabbage and 2,000 years of cooking experience."

"Yours?"

"No. I'm only forty-two. The Chinese Mandarins—or their slaves."

"And this?"

"It's called sour hot soup."

Steve had actually tidied up his living-room by shifting all his papers, his typewriter and other flotsam on to the bed. Two candles stuck in gin bottles were reflected in the table and from the foil tops of Czech Pilsner beer and a bottle of champagne which was wallowing in his biggest saucepan in water and ice from the fridge.

"Have I gate-crashed?" Mary asked.

"Explain yourself." Steve put the dishes down and went out for the rice and soup.

"I wondered," she said, "whether all this romantic set up was not more for one of your one-meal girls. After all we have been more than friends for six months. Why the soft lights and sweet music?"

"It's me birthday, that's why. But now we can use the occasion to celebrate your new job. Also, I have something serious to talk to you about."

"Farewell party?" Mary kept her voice cool but felt her stomach sink.

"I hope not." He started to serve the rice.

He had shed his apron. She looked at him, the supposedly tough, cynical, caustic crime reporter who was on first name terms with the top men in Scotland Yard and with the bosses of the Soho mobs. Larger, better looking, well dressed men feared him as a professional rival and wondered how he always had the company of beautiful and intelligent women.

He was quiet, but his quietness was of a kind which looked as though it could make trouble if disturbed. He was a man people hesitated to pick a quarrel with.

His attractiveness to women was no mystery. He was male but pathetically unable to cope. In his work he had flair and thoroughness, but he forgot to eat. Or he ate horrible café food. He drank too much. He did not bother about clothes. He was a man to mother, to dominate and to be dominated by.

When the silence had gone on too long, Mary said: "This beef and orange peel is simply incredible." She took more.

Another long silence grew in the room.

"The point is," Steve said in an unusual voice, as though he felt somewhat ashamed of it, "I've been wondering whether I shouldn't start thinking about getting married."

So that was it. It took Mary several seconds to recover from the shock and a few more to think of something to say.

"Who is the lucky little woman?" she asked. "Do you have anyone in particular in view for this honour?"

"I suppose I must sound like one of your ghastly reader's letters. Actually this is something that has happened only since I met you. Anyway, you know that."

Mary stared at him, slowing shaking her head.

"Of course," he said, "I know there's the age difference. I'm forty-two and you are twenty-six. But these days. . . ."

Mary shook her head again, pityingly.

"And I suppose that I should now go down on my knees and thank your lordship—not for proposing marriage—no no—that would be far too definite but for offering a girl hope that one day—one glorious day—he might actually propose. Pah!" she finished.

Steve had stopped eating and was staring into his rice bowl.

"Am I really such a swine?" he asked.

"You're not a swine at all, darling," she said with gentle venom. "You are just a bachelor and, as you said, forty-two. That requires explaining."

"What?"

"How a normal male can reach your age without marrying. Selfishness, that's all it is. Selfishness and a rotten attitude to women."

From inside his cupped hands, Steve said: "All I said was that I wanted to stop being a bachelor."

Mary snorted: "And I suppose you think that is only a matter of deciding to Give Up Your Liberty. It's the quality that made you a bachelor which will almost certainly stop you from being a good husband. I would have no more confidence in an elderly bachelor as a husband than in a soldier with glasses."

"Not elderly," Steve groaned.

"Getting on. But you tell me: How do you explain the fact that you prefer sleeping all round the town and that you never got married?"

He shrugged his shoulders, lifted his hands helplessly and let them drop.

"That would be a job for a psychologist. I suppose that when I was at the usual age for that kind of thing it was the end of the war. Hiroshima and all that. A brave new world with the atom bomb hanging over it."

"That kind of thing," Mary quoted mockingly. "Pure rationalization. You were in no different position from all the other millions. Anyway, what has happened since then to change your mind?" She threw the evening paper to him. "Look at the splash."

Right across the top of the page in heavy sanserif it said: "VOLKSBOMB FOR BONN?"

It went on: "A decisive step toward the arming of West

Germany with strategic nuclear weapons was taken yesterday in London.

"Politicians and businessmen from Britain, West Germany and Holland have agreed on three-power collaboration in the gas centrifuge method of producing enriched uranium—the substance used to fire the hydrogen bomb."

Steve groaned. "That's all we need. Plain madness."

"Worse than madness," Mary said. "You should hear my father on the subject. He was a war prisoner. 'Let them have so much as a knife,' he says, 'and they'll use it to get a pistol and before you can turn round they'll be armed to the teeth and starting the third world war'."

"Nothing we can do about it though," Steve said.

Mary shrugged: "Let's stick to the point. How could I marry a man who wonders whether he shouldn't think about marrying me because he supposes he's fallen in love with me?"

"I do love you, Mary," he said.

She got out a handkerchief and dabbed the corner of an eye. Steve moved round the table and kissed her.

She pressed him away but took his hand and held it in silence when he sat down again.

"I'll open the champagne," he said.

"No don't. Save it for another time. Let's go to the pub for a drink and I'll go home from there."

In the pub she said: "I feel a right cow for not coming back with you on your birthday but I simply have to go home."

"Do you really? You're a big girl now."

"It's Dad. I had a letter this morning, posted in East Berlin. He said he'd be flying home from there yesterday. I suppose there was some hold-up and he'll be back today. I simply must be there after not seeing him for so long."

It was eighteen minutes past ten but the clock in the Brewer's Arms had just struck the half hour and Harry Brown, the last publican left in Fleet Street according to Steve, had turned on his secret weapon. Harry Brown according to himself, lived a miserable existence between a harridan wife, the brewers and journaliste. Journalists, he said, were harder to detach from a bar than limpets from a rock—hence the secret weapon, which consisted of turning the juke box up to its highest pitch. Not even journalists could stand more than about ten minutes of the ear-splitting noise. Smiling gently, Harry polished glasses and watched his customers screaming at each other above the din.

"Have you writ a good piece?" he shouted across three feet of space to where Mary sat in the corner of the bar reading the first edition of the *Phoenix*.

She spun the paper round on the bar top and he peered over to read, still polishing.

"What It Is Like to Be the Other Woman," the headline said and the blurb told the customers that Mary Penny offered them the exclusive, authentic story about how film star Dawn Fair had felt as the unmarried wife of her director who was barred by the Catholic Church from getting divorced.

"Nicely got up load of old rope about a burning issue," Harry yelled. "I like your picture though."

"It's always nice to read your own stuff in print. I suppose your clock's twelve minutes fast as usual?"

He nodded.

"Steve may just make it. Stand him up a double Johnnie Walker and what'll you have?"

As he began to say: "I'll have a . . ." his thin-faced wife came behind the bar and he changed to: "Not for me, dear, I've got a Cola here." His wife cleared some plates and took them out and Harry instantly held his glass under the whisky dispenser with a broad wink at Mary.

A moment later Steve burst through the door, winced at the din and pushed through to where Mary sat.

"Clairvoyant, that's us," Harry said. "It's standing on the bar. Paid for," he added, as Steve felt for money.

"Cheers." He downed the whisky in one and said: "Slip me another, Harry. Haven't had one all evening."

"Have you got to go in again, Steve," Mary asked. "There's something I want to talk to you about."

"Sorry, darling. They're going to splash the Heath murder and I've got to rewrite it. I'll be free by midnight. Have you eaten?"

She shook her head.

"How about Nick's at twelve, then?"

He hurried out.

Nick's was always crowded at this time of night but Mary squeezed in between a photo agency messenger and a big cheerful man from her own process department who was demolishing a steak with two eggs on top, chips and several slices of bread. Nick's was famous in Fleet Street for big portions, good quality, speed and cheapness.

Just before midnight the door banged and Steve thrust his way past the long counter calling out as he went: "Ham, two eggs, chips, two slices and tea."

"No wonder you can't get your trousers to meet at the top," Mary said, making way for him to sit on the seat she had kept against all comers.

"You feature writers have it made," he complained. "That's my lunch, tea and dinner in one. I've been running like a dog all day on this Heath murder and now I've still got to ring the Yard every half hour or so in case anything breaks before the last replate."

"Oh, no, Steve. We haven't seen each other for a week."

"And you weren't very nice to me then." He raised the cheap fork, loaded with steaming ham and eggs to his mouth. "What's on your mind, duck?" he said.

"It's my father." She turned her black eyes on him, filled with worry.

"What, hasn't he shown up yet?"

"No. And he hasn't written, wired or phoned. I feel sure something's wrong."

Steve chewed slowly and said: "He wrote to you last from East Berlin. What date should he have been back?"

"He wrote on the eleventh and said he'd be coming on a plane from Schoenefeld on the next day."

"Where's Shurner . . . what's its name?"

"It's the East Berlin airport."

"What the hell was he doing over there in Communist Germany?"

"I haven't the slightest idea. He wrote me a few times from West Germany and then from West Berlin. Chatty stuff but he didn't say what he was doing. He had just arranged with his partner to take six months off to travel and recuperate. After he got that money, you know. All that Mr. Crabtree has had from him—that's his partner—has been a couple of postcards."

Steve thought a moment. "You've tried the airline?"

"Yes. They contacted East Berlin airport and were told that there had been a booking in that name but it had not been taken up."

"People change their minds."

"I'm sure he'd have let me know if he could."

"If he could!" Steve said. "You think it's serious?"

Mary nodded miserably. "I keep thinking of him lying in

some hospital unable to identify himself. Or even dead. He could have had an accident."

Steve patted her hand. "Now, now, my love. Don't let your imagination run away with you. That sort of thing could happen here, but when people are abroad they carry their passports. The first thing that would happen would be that the British authorities would be informed. Maybe that's where we should start from. Why didn't you ring the Foreign Office?"

"I thought of that. But I reckoned that if I went there some snooper from the press would latch on to it. You know what kind of a mountain they can fudge up out of a molehill. Especially with East Berlin involved. Briton Detained Behind Iron Curtain. That kind of thing."

"Maybe he is."

"Oh, Steve." Her lips trembled.

"We can't rule it out. You've no idea what your old man was doing. Perhaps he wants to lie low for some reason. It would be a way: cross into East Berlin post you a letter, book a flight to London, cross back into West Berlin. Trail ends."

Steve pushed away the remnants of his ham and eggs with distaste.

Mary said: "No, Steve. Dad wouldn't do a thing like that to me. He would know I would worry and start making enquiries."

Steve lit a cigarette and sat thinking.

"Any address on the letter?"

"No. It was a piece of paper torn out of a cheap notebook. I've got it at home."

The café door opened and a youth with terrible acne came in, looked round, spotted Steve and called: "Mr. Blake. Mr. Gibbons is going mad on the news desk. There's been a P.A.

flash. They've got the Heath murderer. He says he's got to replate at once."

Steve groaned. "You can't even get a meal in this game. O.K. Tell Gibbons to keep all the tape. I'll be right up."

He stood up. "Pay my bill, Mary, and get a taxi home. I'll come to your place as soon as I can get done. I'll get Tom Westbury, our diplomatic correspondent, to find out what he can at the Foreign Office. Strict secrecy. Don't worry about that side."

He hurried to the door and turned. "By the way, what's your father's first name."

"Harold." As the door was closing she shouted: "Viner, of course."

For all its steel and glass tile, the new Scotland Yard building seemed to have imported from the Embankment to Broadway that inevitable police and prison odour in which carbolic and stale sweat play their vital part.

There was also something of the hospital about its endless corridors of white and black squares lined with identical doors. Mary felt herself going tiptoe. Her escort stopped at one of the doors and knocked, opened it without waiting and showed her in.

Under the desk facing the door she saw a pair of large, round-toed shoe soles. On the desk was a large hand. Nothing else was visible for a moment until a big shoulder and a face rose above the edge of the desk. It was a formidable face.

"Dropped my ballpoint," the man said.

"Inspector Gullet?"

"That's me. And you are Miss Mary Penny, eh? I told your blackmailing pal Blake that I'd give you ten minutes. And I wouldn't have done that except that my missus is a fan of yours. It'll make her day if I tell her I've met you."

"I'm glad she likes my stuff."

Mary dived into her handbag and came up with a round tin. "Steve said it's no use offering you a cigarette so he sent you a tin of tobacco—St. Bruno—and hoped you'd smoke it with his compliments." She put it on the desk.

Gullet looked as though he might smile if such a thing were possible. "Bribery," he said, and added ponderously : "I could put you under arrest for that."

"It would be a pleasure," Mary said. "But Steve always said he wished everyone he had to deal with at the Yard were a Gullet." Even as she heard herself saying it, it sounded corny, but he seemed to wallow in it. Feed 'em what they want to hear—whether it's Mr. or Mrs. Gullet. It made her feel ashamed.

"Steve told you about Daddy?" That Daddy stuff always went down with his type.

He nodded. "Wrote you from East Berlin and nothing heard since. Did Blake get anywhere with the Foreign Office?"

"Nothing has been reported to them."

"It's very tricky. Nobody wants this kind of case. East Germany doesn't exist. It's a hole in the map as far as we are concerned. I cannot have any direct contact with East Germany. That's the first difficulty."

"But I could. I could cross the border."

He leaned back and struggled to fish his pipe out of his pocket again. "Filthy habit," he commented, filling it from his new tin of tobacco. "And then suppose you got knocked off as an accomplice of your father, supposing that he's been knocked off there? I wouldn't advise doing that."

"If that's the first difficulty, what's the next one?"

He puffed a cloud of blue smoke out and tamped his pipe with a forefinger slightly blackened by long burning and said: "It's no crime to disappear. Any person, as far as I'm concerned can disappear as much as he likes. Crime is my business."

"But my father . . ." Mary stopped. "Of course, you don't know him. I'm sure. . . ."

"Whatever you may believe, Miss Penny, doesn't cut any ice. As far as I am concerned, your father may just not want to have his whereabouts known. He may be involved in a business deal or an affair of some kind. Anything. He's a grown man. He hasn't committed any known crime or been the victim of one. Imagine where we would be if we had to follow up every erring husband or wife or every businessman who wants to stay incognito."

"You don't know my father."

Gullet sighed. "It's not the point. I am an official. Officially there's nothing I can do."

"But . . . isn't there anything you can do unofficially? Steve thought. . . ."

"I know what Steve thinks: I scratch his back and he scratches mine. I like to keep in with the press and they with me. But there are limits. This involves the Foreign Office."

Mary put her face into her hands. Her long dark hair flowed past her wrists and she looked the picture of despair. Peering through her fingers she could see that this suited Gullet. Any minute now she would get up and go and leave him to read his In tray.

Instead, she said: "Well, if Scotland Yard is so powerless, I'll go and tell my editor and then I'll just go to East Berlin. Maybe if I disappear too you'll do something."

Gullet poked the tobacco down in his pipe, burnt his finger, cursed silently and wiped it on his trouser leg and said: "I didn't say there was nothing to be done. Anyway, let me have the particulars and I'll think it over."

"Oh, will you really." Her head came up, eyes shining with gratitude. "What do you want to know?"

"What's your father's full name?"

"Harold Viner."

"Not Penny?"

"No. My real name is Mary Penelope Viner, my paper thought Mary Penny sounded better."

"What's his age?"

"Fifty-three."

"Have you brought the letter he posted in East Berlin?"

"I Xeroxed it. Here's a copy for you to keep."

Gullet looked at the copies of the envelope and letter.

"Envelope dated Berlin B, 11.10.68. 15. Fifteen hours. It must have been posted before three in the afternoon. Simply that he will be flying next day to London. Had he been to East Berlin before?"

"Not that I know of."

"Speak German?"

"Very well. He was a POW in Germany. Married a German. I speak it well too, because of that."

"POW, speaks German, disappears in East Berlin. Opens up possibilities, doesn't it?"

"What kind?"

"Obvious. Anyway, it's no use speculating. Do you know where he was staying in West Berlin?"

She reached down into her handbag. "This is his last letter from West Berlin. Headed notepaper. Pension Ebert, Bleibtreustrasse. He usually stayed in pensions because they're cheaper."

"And where can I find you?"

"I live at my father's house. I stayed on since mother died though I'd sooner be nearer my job. It's in N.W.3."

She gave him her card. When he stood up he seemed short

for a policeman but powerful looking with arms and shoulders that stretched the sleeves and shoulders of his jacket. In spite of age and overweight not a man to tussle with. She got up too.

"Well, Miss Viner, or Penny, the most I can do is to put through a simple inquiry to the West Berlin police asking if they have any knowledge of your father's whereabouts."

"That's wonderful of you, Inspector. You've no idea what a relief it is. Will it take long?"

"Three days, a week. Might be more. I'll see that you are told whenever we know anything."

At the door she scribbled on another card, her business card, Mary Penny of the *Phoenix*. "Give that to your wife, please," she said.

He turned it over. "Your husband is a darling," it said.

"Soft soap," Gullet commented, unable to hide his pleasure.

TWO

SHADOWED

FOR cheapness she chose a small hotel out near Kaiserdamm but still only fifteen minutes by U-Bahn to Kurfürstendamm. Her room on the first floor was small and clean with a wash-basin and hot and cold water.

The speech of the Consul's secretary was a battlefield be-tween plain London and refined. Nobody was in the Consul's room but the sound of water came from behind a door. A plaque on the desk said: Mrs. Patricia MacDermott. Of course, there had been that row about appointing a woman consul to West Berlin. In one corner of her brain the idea registered that here was a ready-made women's story. Our Woman in West Berlin. Ugh!

Mrs. MacDermott came in from washing, flapping long hands to complete the drying process. Coolly hospitable she came forward holding out her hand and at the same time apologizing for doing so.

"Continental habit. It becomes quite automatic after a time. One takes it back to England for a time and people find it very curious. Nice of you to call. Shall we have some coffee?

"Of course you've come about your father, my dear. I had an enquiry from the F.O. But we know nothing at all. You must be absolutely frantic. You can be sure I'll do anything I can."

This seemed to be the introduction to a long statement

about what she could not do. It included nearly everything. In fact the British police had done all that she could have done as consul—asked the West German police to make enquiries.

"Routine enquiries, though."

"I do so agree, Miss Viner. But what else could they do? There's not the least reason to suppose that any crime has been committed from the standpoint of the police here. An Englishman has disappeared or is said to have disappeared. What concern is that of theirs?"

"Can't the British military authorities help?"

Mrs. MacDermott smiled patiently and even kindly.

"The British military presence"—she managed to put the word into inverted commas—"in West Berlin has come to be regarded as relating mainly to international matters. Power politics if you like. You have only to look at the map. West Berlin is well over a hundred miles from West Germany. It is surrounded by the Communists. This is why the British, American and French troops are here. But local matters are none of the business of the occupation forces. West Berlin is governed by the Senate. It has its own police and laws."

"And the West Berlin authorities aren't interested."

The consul laughed and put a cool hand on Mary's wrist.

"My dear, all they have done till now is to respond in a routine manner to a routine request from Scotland Yard. Who can say how they will respond to a request from a young and, may I say, remarkably beautiful woman? And a foreigner at that. Why not try your charm?"

"Well, I suppose. . . ." Mary looked down at the woman's hand still on her wrist. The older woman looked too, patted the wrist and took her hand away.

"One thing I can do for you, Miss Viner," she said, "is to

call up the chief of the detective force here and ask him to see you. Quite unofficially, you know. Shall I do that?"

"It's very kind of you."

"Nothing at all, my dear."

She went to the desk and pressed the intercom. "Get me Herr Karl-Heinz Staengel at the Kriminal Polizei, please."

She came back and sat down again.

"Do you think I should go and see the people in East Berlin?" Mary asked.

Mrs. MacDermott gave this long consideration. "Officially I cannot advise you to do so. We have no official connections of any sort with them, but there are a few British people of a kind over there, working, studying and so on."

The phone rang. "Ah, Herr Staengel." Mrs. MacDermott spoke rapidly in good German. Without knowing what was said at the other end, Mary had a feeling that Herr Staengel either knew she was in West Berlin or was expecting her to be.

"Very nice of you," Mrs. MacDermott said. "Then I'll tell her three o'clock."

She put the phone down and wrote on a piece of paper.

"He will see you at three," she translated for Mary. "This is the address."

"It really is kind of you," Mary said.

Mrs. MacDermott shook her head. "Now what were we talking about? Going over the border. Well, you can cross at any time, using your British passport. You are restricted to East Berlin. Once you are over the border you are no longer in my jurisdiction. That means that a British passport gives you no protection. Therefore I can't advise you to go."

"But plenty of people do go?"

"Hundreds. Thousands. Every day sightseeing buses leave West Berlin and tour East Berlin. It is perfectly normal.

Nothing ever happens. But your case is not the same. You have some impression that your father may have disappeared there. It is no secret that Berlin is one of the world centres of espionage and smuggling. Who knows what your father might have been doing or been thought to have been doing? If there is something of that kind, you might also be involved."

Mary said: "It seems perfectly natural to me that a girl would try to find out what had happened to her father."

"Natural, certainly. Commendable. On the other hand there might be people who would think you were an accomplice in what he might have been engaged in. It could appear like that to suspicious people. I cannot help you if you get into difficulties over there."

She got up and Mary followed her example.

"Bonn would get absolutely furious if we had anything to do with those people at all. It's comical really, considering that Bonn does more trade with East Germany than any Western country."

In her experience, policemen were large, crude, domineering men like Gullet. Herr Karl-Heinz Staengel was small and slight, not taller than herself and looking as though he weighed less. He looked wiry and hard. He came across the thick fitted carpet holding out his right hand and crinkling his ice-blue eyes in a smile that scarcely reached his thin chops and straight-edged mouth. His iron grey hair was crew cut. Somewhere between forty-five and sixty, Mary decided, declining coffee and cognac as she sat down.

His desk was empty but for phones, intercom and a file with a piece of paper clipped to it on which was written "Viner".

He caught her glance and said: "Fraulein Viner, I sent for the file about your father after Mrs. MacDermott telephoned. I have also discussed it with the officer who made the investigation. It is a problem what to say.

"At the Ebert Pension, it seems, Herr Viner paid his bill and said he would not be needing the room that night as he would be leaving Berlin that day."

He opened the file.

"That would be October 11. He left his bag there, saying he would pick it up later."

Staengel closed the file. "Just before ten there was a telephone call and someone with a foreign accent, who said he was Herr Viner, and was assumed by the hotel porter to be him, said that he had no time to collect his bag as he had something to do and he would send a messenger who would identify himself by presenting Herr Viner's passport and collect the suitcase. It seemed a very normal matter and the porter gave it no thought until our investigator called. And that was all."

"Yes," Mary said. "I heard all that from Inspector Gullet. Is there something more that can be done?"

He turned on his thin smile again for a moment and said : "Naturally I thought you had not come to hear what you already know. Since Mrs. MacDermott telephoned I have been squeezing my brains to think what more could be done. But in fact, Fraulein Viner, nothing can be done, short of a full-scale man-hunt."

"I can't believe that nothing can be done," Mary burst out.

"I understand your feelings," Staengel said. "But please try to see the difficulties. There is no ground so far for believing that any crime has been committed. To involve my force in the expense and time for a major search, especially now with all the unrest that there is in West Berlin, is simply not to be considered. And anything less would not produce results but would simply waste time."

He held out his hands palms out inviting her understanding. She shook her head.

"I am sure that there is something that could be done."

"Not if we are realistic. People who are neither criminal nor involved in any criminal activity are disappearing all the time—mostly because they are tired of their wives or husbands or of routine jobs. We are neither empowered nor do we have the means to chase them up at the request of relatives and friends."

"I know all that but it does not apply to my father. He would never do anything that would worry me. I am sure that something has happened to him."

Herr Staengel held up a well kept hand. "Please believe that I realize how worried you are. It is because of this and because you are British, a nation for which I have only respect, that I have seen you personally to explain. I met Inspector Gullet when I was in London for a police conference. That is another reason why I have in fact exceeded my duty already in this matter—unhappily without result. Believe me, there is no more I can do. Please come and see me at any time you have reason to believe that some crime has been committed in West Berlin. Just call me up."

He dropped his card on the table in front of her.

Mary got out at Wittenberg Place in order to walk down to Kurfürstendamm.

What to do next? Obviously she must call at the Ebert Pension. She walked down to Bleibtreustrasse and spoke to the proprietress. Frau Reingold was unhelpful. No, the porter had gone away soon after the police came and asked questions. She knew no more than he had told the police. And she made it very clear that she did not want to know anything.

Mary walked back, window shopping. It was too late to go to East Berlin even if she had made her mind up to do that. She was glad to be able to put off the decision. It could wait till morning.

It must have been after one when she awoke and wondered why.

There was a knock at her door.

"Who is it?" she called in German.

"Ssh. Don't put the light on. It's me. Steve."

"No! Oh, Steve, darling."

"Ssh. Quick."

He came in fast and locked the door behind him. She clung to him and kissed him till he was breathless.

"Steve, darling. Am I glad to see you? What are you doing here?"

"We'll talk about it later. I suppose you haven't got a drink? No, you wouldn't have. I could certainly do with one now. I suppose it will do me good to go without."

"How did you find me? How did you get in here?"

"Stop asking idiotic questions. I'm here." He put his arm round her. "I love you."

She kissed him again. "Did you come all the way from London to tell me that?"

"Partly. Mainly to see that you didn't get into trouble. Well?"

"Well, what?"

"I said, I love you. How do you feel about it?"

"Oh, Steve. I simply adore you. How did you get in here? How did you know I was here anyway?"

He laughed. "You didn't think I was any good at the practical crime stuff, eh? What would you have done?"

"I wouldn't know where to begin."

"I took a room in the Ebert Pension, knowing that you would show up there some time. I insisted on a front room looking on to the street and I sat there glued to the window like a bedridden bachelor and waited for you to show up. Well, you did. This afternoon." He was suddenly very quiet and serious. "I've been wondering how to break it to you."

"Break what?"

"The news."

"Is it about Dad?"

"No, you."

"Come, Steve, I can take it."

"Well, I was sitting there and I saw you come along. You looked simply incredible on those long legs. And I was just about to rush down and get a half-nelson on you when I noticed something."

He stopped.

"What was it? Something in the street?"

"Mary. You were being followed."

"How did you know?"

"Well, I saw you come round the corner and then I saw a bloke come to the same corner, watching you, and as soon as you turned into the pension he lit a cigarette and stood around waiting."

"My God, Steve. Who was it?"

"How the devil should I know. He looked like some goon."

"Why didn't you come down and tell me?"

"Two good reasons. I had to make sure. That meant waiting to see if he really was a tail. I could hardly find that out walking along with you.

"The second reason was that if I had given you an idea of it, you would have had no time to react and you'd have given the game away."

Mary gave him an admiring kiss. "I really am glad you're

here, Steve darling. I would simply have run down and jumped at you."

"Don't get too pleased with yourself. We are now playing in the top league it seems to me. And we aren't equipped for it."

"Go on, Steve."

"I waited till you popped out and then it was clear. He took off after you and I after both. I hope you had a good meal. It took long enough. My stomach is at this minute knocking against my backbone. Not to mention my thirst. Then of course you have to go to a cinema. I dared not go away to get a snack or a drink in case they changed guard. And sure enough they did. The first goon was relieved by a new one. A nasty little whippet-like type with a leather cap. That one kept you company all the way here. So did I. Shortly after you came in, I asked for a room. No baggage, so cash in advance. Signing on I saw your room number and here I am."

"Thank God," Mary said.

"I suppose he's still out there," Steve remarked.

Holding his hand in the dark, Mary asked: "What do you reckon it's about, Steve? Is it the police, do you think? I was there this afternoon."

"Can't rule it out. Maybe they think you'll lead them to your Pa. Maybe it's people from East Berlin; but the opposition, whoever they are, aren't in this thing for fun. It takes men and money to keep a tag even on one person. And look how quickly they got on to you."

They sat silently in the darkened room.

Mary said after a while: "I've made up my mind to go over to East Berlin tomorrow." She waited for the arguments and prepared to counter them, but none came. "It was wonderful of you to come, Steve," she said after a moment.

B

"So wonderful that I hate to sound ungrateful. But I must tell you that you don't have to get involved. It's my business and . . . well . . . it's my business. He's my father, not yours. And as you say, things are apparently serious. I don't want to get you in a mess Steve, but I can't go back unless I've tried to do all I can."

He picked up her hand and kissed it very gently, running his lips all over it, folding it and rubbing her knuckles against his closed eyes.

"Why did you come, Steve?"

"For the same reason as you. I had to come."

She turned to him and burst into tears against his coat.

"Ssh. Ssh. Darling. No weeping. There isn't time."

She laughed as she wept. "Don't stop me. Steve. What is nicer than to cry for happiness? I almost don't mind being followed by a goon."

She stooped soon and said: "Do you think he's still there," getting up to have a look.

Steve pulled her back.

"Don't touch the curtains. They mustn't know you know. Also they mustn't know about me. Tomorrow, you will keep the goon busy, behaving like an ordinary journalist. I am not being tailed so I shall go and try to find things out in East Berlin."

Steve went on the S-Bahn, the Berlin elevated railway which operates in both parts of Berlin but by some anomaly normal to the divided city, belongs entirely to the East Berlin authorities.

In the station at East Berlin it was like any international border, with passport control, customs and exchange offices. And even, he noticed, tax free shops.

He cleared passports and customs, changed a pound into

East marks and approached a green uniformed officer. It was eight o'clock.

Three hours and nine officials later, an official car took him to the office of the Public Prosecutor where a young man led him through the entrance, and along ancient corridors to a door bearing the name Dr. Eugen Ginglass.

Inside the room was a large desk and the walls were lined with steel files. A short, plump bespectacled man came to meet him holding out his hand.

"Ginglass," he said. It was a disappointment. He pronounced it with a hard "G". "I hear that you are concerned with learning something about Mr. Viner."

"I'm here on behalf of his daughter."

"Come this way."

He spoke good English but with a very strong accent. A door opened into a smaller room with a round table surrounded by uncomfortable looking armchairs. Coffee cups stood on the table and—good God—a bottle of Scotch.

"I hope you like Yonnie Valker whisky," Ginglass said.

"I was weaned on it," Steve breathed as Ginglass sloshed a good three fingers into each glass. A girl came in with coffee.

"Please do not be offended, Mr. Blake, but do you have any way of proving that you represent Mr. Viner's daughter?"

Steve fished in his pocket. He put a photo-copy of Viner's letter from East Berlin on the desk and a note that Mary had written that morning—To Whom It May Concern.

Ginglass studied them.

"What is your personal interest in these matters?" he asked, handing the papers back.

"Well, you see, Mary and I . . . er, we have a sort of understanding . . . sort of engaged. She's very worried about her father."

"Yes. I had been wondering when he would come to see me again."

He coughed and sat silently for a while. "You see, Mr. Blake, I have to be careful. Now that I know that Mr. Viner has not reappeared, I see that there might be people interested in finding out whether he gave us any information and what it was. When did you arrive in West Berlin?"

"The day before yesterday."

"And you speak no German?"

"No."

"Why did not Miss Viner come herself?"

Steve hesitated. He could hardly say: because if you people have knocked Viner off you might grab her as well.

Finally he said: "I had business in Berlin so it seemed best for me to come here as well."

There was another long wait.

"Good," Ginglass said, his mind apparently made up. "Mr. Viner came to see me on October 11. He had a very interesting story. He said that he was on the track of a former SS officer who had been a guard in Sachsenhausen Concentration Camp, not far from Berlin, in the little town of Oranienburg. A score or two British war prisoners were kept there at various times, including Mr. Viner.

"One of the SS guards at the camp was Wolfgang Kessel, a peculiarly perverted kind of sadist. Mr. Viner happened to be the only English Jew in the camp and Kessel singled him out as a special victim."

He stopped and said: "I think we should have a drink."

The Scotch went down like milk. Ginglass looked surprised as he put down his scarcely touched glass. But he poured another long one for Steve.

"Your native schnapps," he said. "Actually I prefer cognac."

Ginglass went on: "I would not like you to think me naïve. I am telling you this because—although it is my duty to be suspicious, and you come without any real credentials—Mr. Viner had already left quite a broad trail in West Berlin. There is little reason to doubt that what I am telling you would not be news if you came from, should we say, the adverse party."

He gave Steve a small grin and Steve took another reasonable mouthful of Scotch.

Ginglass went steadily on: "I am something of a specialist on the Sachsenhausen Camp. I am a Jew. Both my parents died in the gas chamber at Sachsenhausen."

He raised a podgy hand and stopped Steve from offering commiseration.

"I can give you the personal history of most of the guards there. In the case of this one, Kessel, neither I nor anyone else bothered to follow him up for the good reason that he was registered as killed with other SS officers in a jeep which was destroyed by a Soviet fighter plane as they were fleeing west of Berlin.

"Since you are British, I hope you won't be offended if I recall that the tendency of these Nazi murderers was to run West rather than be captured by the Russians. Some of them believed that the western powers would join forces with them to smash Russia at the last moment. Nobody can say they had no reason."

Dr. Ginglass opened a file on the table and took out an envelope. He threw a small booklet over to Steve.

"That is the identity document of Kessel, bloodstained, as you see, which was found on a burned body in the jeep, and a report of his death. The blood group tattooed under his arm also tallied with that on his papers.

"Mr. Viner said that he knew all about that and had also

believed Kessel to be dead but that he now knew differently. He said he knew for a fact that Kessel was still alive and living under another name in West Germany or West Berlin.

"He seemed suspicious of us, though a little less so when he found that I was Jewish too.

"He was very nervous. He had been making enquiries in West Germany and West Berlin and he felt that he was in danger. He was being followed and considered that his life was threatened. What he wanted from us was help in finding out everything we could about Kessel's past. Maybe we had a pre-war file on the man. He said that Kessel had lived in Dresden for some time and according to another Sachsenhausen prisoner, had been in gaol there.

"If that were true, of course, there might well be fingerprints recorded, and this would be absolutely conclusive proof that the man whom Mr. Viner suspected of being Kessel was in fact so.

"I was quite unable to persuade him to tell us the name of the man he suspected of being Kessel. He said he was afraid of a leakage before everything was investigated. He said the man occupied a very high position and was powerful enough to shrug off anything but cast-iron proof."

"Bloody silly," Steve said. "If he really thought that someone might try to put him out of the way. It would be an even greater temptation if they thought that he had not passed the information on." But Ginglass's story would be a clever one if in fact Viner had been kept in East Germany.

"Just what I told him," Ginglass said. "But he said he had taken steps to see that what he knew would come out if anything happened to him."

"Do you think anything has?"

Ginglass shrugged. "I know no more than you. I told Mr. Viner that I would have a general search made for Kessel's background with special emphasis in Dresden and let him know if anything was turned up. He gave me his London address. He then said that he intended to make an 'English departure' from Berlin."

Steve cocked an eye inquiringly.

"It's what you call French leave. He wanted to leave secretly in fact. So he said that he had left his bag in his hotel in West Berlin, after paying his bill, and said he would call for it later. Actually he intended to abandon it because he thought that the people who were on his trail would assume that he was there as long as his bag was in the hotel. There was nothing special in it. But he was nervous that they would watch the airport.

"So I suggested that the best thing would be not to go back to West Berlin at all. He could fly from Schoenefeld. All he had to do was book a ticket to London. The ticket would be a visa to take him through the border to Schoenefeld airport and he could stay overnight in East Berlin, instead of finding a new hotel in West Berlin.

"I sent a messenger with him to buy a ticket and book him a room in the Johannishof Hotel, where he registered. But he didn't stay there. He went out in the early evening and did not come back. We paid the hotel bill. I assumed that he had got nervous and suspicious and had gone back to West Berlin."

"Couldn't that be checked? They seem to have a very thorough records system at the city border."

"It was checked." He consulted another file.

"Here it is. A British subject, Harold Viner, Passport Number 27685741, entered East Berlin at 9.45 a.m. on October 11, through the Friedrichstrasse crossing point and left by the same crossing point at 9.15 p.m. on the same day."

Steve looked grim. So the trail went right back to West Berlin. The question was: was it a trail or a red herring?

"And he didn't come back into East Berlin on the next day, October 12, the day he was scheduled to fly?"

"No," Ginglass answered. "I naturally checked that. He did not. But I found out something else though I don't know whether it has any importance. Mr. Viner also visited East Berlin for a few hours on October 9—two days before he came to see me. I have no idea why, or where he went. He did not mention it to me and I would not have known unless I had asked the border authorities to make a complete check. You may be sure that these are the only two occasions that he was in East Berlin since the border was closed. Before that time we had no records."

Steve asked: "Did you go ahead with your enquiries about this SS man—Kessel?"

"They are still going on. It takes a lot of time to work through all those old police files. I may get news at any time —or none at all. But you may be sure that I will keep up the pressure. They say here that I am mad about Sachsenhausen. It has indeed become something of an obsession with me. A labour of hate, should we say."

Steve felt in his pocket for Mary's cards and gave him one.

"It's the same address as Mr. Viner's. Will you let her know about anything that turns up?"

"Of course. And will you do the same for me?"

Back in West Berlin, he still had hours to kill before he could go to Mary's room. He went to a Western. Even if it was crazy to hear cowboys talking German, the language of the guns was international.

Steve slid silently into Mary's room and turned the key after him. She was sitting in the armchair reading by the faint light shed by an electric torch stood on its base on the floor and shining on the ceiling.

"Thank God you're back Steve," she whispered. "It's been hell waiting and wondering what might have happened."

She picked up a bottle from the floor. "No errors this time," she said, pouring him a Scotch.

He laughed and pulled a bottle from his pocket. "Two minds, eh."

"And here are rolls, ham and cheese. Now tell me, how did you get on?"

"You're lucky to see me back. The skirts in East Berlin are much shorter than in West Berlin."

"Shut up, Steve. Tell me."

"We've only got their word for all that," Mary said.

"I've had the same idea working away in the back of my tiny brain. Suppose they have picked him up and don't want it known. It's just the sort of story to make up—that Kessel stuff—border records showing that he went out. Who can prove anything?"

"I hadn't got that far but it's what I meant. But still, Wolfgang Kessel did exist and I know that Dad hates his guts. I feel sure that if he knew Kessel were alive he would try to do something about it."

"Moreover, as a story it seems over-complicated if it isn't true. All they would need to say would be that he had come and gone like thousands do every day. Nobody at the border asks why people come."

"So we're back to square one. He did come back to West Berlin and so I suppose he did phone the pension and send for his bag. And there the trail ends."

Mary sat slumped, thinking.

Then she stubbed her cigarette, drank her Scotch and said as though trying to convince herself: "It's a job for the police. What the hell are all these coppers for? I'm going to see

Staengel again in the morning. I'll tell him about Kessel, make him see that it's a case with overtones."

Looking very uneasy, Steve rubbed his chin for a long time.

"You don't seem to agree."

"There was something I didn't tell you," he said reluctantly. "I mentioned to Ginglass that I thought of calling on the chief of detectives in West Berlin.

" 'Karl-Heinz Staengel,' he says, very pat.

"Then he walked over to a filing cabinet and took out a folder, a very thick one. He put it down in front of me. It was labelled Staengel, Karl-Heinz.

" 'Being in German it won't mean much to you,' he said, 'but briefly: Herr Staengel was an SS major. As a lieutenant, he was for a short time also a guard at the Sachsenhausen Concentration Camp. Later as a major, he served on the SS staff in Budapest, during the liquidation of the Hungarian Jews'."

"If that's true," I said, "why don't you publish it?"

" 'We have',", he told me. 'Along with hundreds of others.'

"Then he said: 'Mr. Blake, what you do is your business, but I would strongly warn you against discussing this matter with Staengel'."

"But I've already done it," Mary said.

"That's right. And then you got a tail. I didn't want to tell Ginglass that."

"You didn't even tell him I was here."

"How could I? If you were, why didn't you go to see him?"

"I can't think of anything else we can do," Mary said.

Steve did not answer. It would be better if the suggestion of going back to London came from her.

THREE

DIETRICH

As though to compensate for its Prussian ugliness as a city, Berlin has possibly the most beautiful surroundings of any capital in the world.

Muggelsee, largest of the vast network of lakes and rivers to the east, is set in lovely forests only half an hour's drive from Friedrichstrasse. There are large tracts of woods so deserted that they provide sanctuary for roe-deer and hares within the city limits.

And for lovers with nowhere else to go.

A little forest pub, the Waldschaenke, between Muggelheim and Rahnsdorf, was the meeting place of Anna Kaul, art student and Wolfram Ackermann, a student of fishery at Rostock on the Baltic Sea. Wolfram was only available every third week on a student's cheap ticket. Sometimes Anna was able to borrow the flat of her friend, but the friend too had a private life to lead, and Anna's parents were old-fashioned.

As usual, they had a few beers and a bockwurst in the Waldschaenke and set out arm in arm into the woods for the place they had named their snuggery. It was a half-submerged bomb shelter or ammunition dump of the Second World War, deep in the forest.

In the summer time, Anna and Wolfram had carried armfuls of pine fronds into the shelter and made a thicky springy couch on the concrete floor. It was dark inside but they knew the way. In the years since the war, thick undergrowth had surrounded the entrance and would give plenty of alarm of any intruder.

Wolfram pushed through first, holding branches from springing back against Anna's face. He bent to go into the bunker door with its two-foot thick lintels and hesitated.

"*Donnerwetter*," he said. "It stinks in here."

Anna came behind him sniffing.

"What is it?"

"Maybe a deer. Crept in here to die."

"Poor thing. It's really horrible though."

"Sit down, darling. I'll take a look."

He took out matches, lit one and went into the bunker, shielding the flame. The bunker was at least 25 yards long and he had to strike several matches."

Suddenly he said in a curious voice: "Get out of here, Anna."

"What. . . ?"

"Get out. I'm coming too."

He followed her into the cold sunshine, bringing up beer and bockwurst.

"We'll have to get the police." He leaned over again but this time nothing came.

"It's a man."

"Dead?" she whispered.

He nodded. "Naked. And his head!"

He took her hand and they ran.

Mary let herself into the Viners' little house in Flask Avenue, Hampstead. It smelt empty. She pushed the door back, with a swathe of letters, papers and circulars, dumped a bag of groceries as she went to the cellar head to turn up the central heating which she had left ticking over during her absence. Then suddenly she remembered and ran back to the door. She riffled through the pile of stuff, looking for the familiar handwriting. There was nothing.

She put the groceries away and sat down to weed out the deposit she had found behind the front door.

The clang of the doorbell startled her. It couldn't be Steve. She had just left him. It might be her father.

Her disappointment must have shown on her face.

The man sensed it and said: "I am sorry. I think you expect someone. I will call another time." His English was good —obviously German but soft and pleasant.

He was tall and it would be difficult to tell his exact age. A sunburned face, bony, lean and deeply lined but youthful, contrasted with grizzled hair. There was an authority and presence in his self-assurance but at the same time he seemed to be trying to put you at ease.

"It's quite all right," Mary said. "What can I do for you?"

"Dietrich," he said and slid off a peccary driving glove with holes in the back. "Franz Dietrich."

Mary took the outstretched hand and said: "Viner." That made the introduction complete.

"I've come about your father.". This time he spoke German. "May I come in."

She moved back.

"What about my father?"

Instead of answering he looked at the windows, back and front. The room ran right through the house. She had not drawn the curtains.

"I think it is a little too public," he smiled. "May I?" He drew the front curtains and then the back.

"I feel insecure sitting in a lighted room when it is dark outside."

"My father?"

"Perhaps I should first tell you something about myself. May I smoke?" He got out a packet of Astors.

"I'm sorry. I must appear rude. You surprised me." She motioned to a chair. "Please sit down and I'll get you a drink. Beer or. . . ?"

"Beer would be nice."

She got it and a gin for herself. He took a drink and sat looking at the tip of his cigarette, turning it round as though trying to make up his mind what to say.

"I am a sort of private investigator," he said. "While you were in Berlin it was not possible for me to make contact with you. I think you know that you were being followed."

She nodded.

"How did you know I was in West Berlin and why should you have made contact with me?"

"I will come to all that. As I said, you were being followed. It was a mistake to go and see Staengel."

"Then it was the police."

"No. It certainly was not the police. As yet I do not know who was behind it."

"It was in any case natural to go to the police."

He sighed. "In West Berlin there is not much that is entirely natural. I mean, especially because of what your father was doing in Berlin, Staengel was the last man to visit."

"Herr Dietrich," Mary said, "I don't know who you are or why you have come to me, but if you have some news of my father, please tell me."

The phone rang. Mary picked it up. "Hallo, darling. Oh, good. I'll have some supper for you in an hour. Just now I have a visitor." She rang off.

"That," said Dietrich with a smile, "was no doubt Mr. Blake. You should tell him that if he wishes to pass unnoticed in West Berlin, he should not go round in an old raincoat and floppy trousers with turn ups."

"Would you mind . . ." Mary began impatiently.

He held up a hand.

"There are many people, some in Germany, others in countries which Hitler occupied, others like your father, who live and work to bring justice to former Nazis who committed crimes against themselves or their families or peoples.

"It was in this way that your father came in touch with me because he needed help in seeking a certain SS officer formerly in Sachsenhausen."

He lit another cigarette and watched the first blue spiral rise.

"Do you know where my father is now?"

"No, I don't. I want to find out. We had arranged to meet in West Berlin but he did not keep the appointment. It may have been that he got close to the quarry and decided that he must disappear for a time. I simply do not know and that is why I am here."

"But you know who he was looking for?"

"Yes. It was a former SS officer named Wolfgang Kessel."

"He imagined that Kessel was dead."

Dietrich nodded. "But he subsequently had reason to think that Kessel was still alive."

"Do you know why he went to Berlin?"

"He did not take me entirely into his confidence. Nor did he tell me that he intended to go to East Berlin?"

"How do you know he did go to East Berlin?"

"That is not the point."

Mary said shortly: "It would be nice to know what the point is, if there is one."

He turned his large blue eyes on her and said: "Miss Viner, I came here because, like you, I have reached a dead end. Your father paid me some money to defray expenses and so on to make some routine investigations. He did not take me into his confidence very much and he did not give me enough information to go on. He gave me the impression that he had a definite idea that a certain person—presumably living under another name—was in fact Kessel. I also got the impression that he felt he would be in some danger if he disclosed his knowledge."

"The only thing that concerns me is to find my father. Can't you possibly suggest anything to be done?"

He said sympathetically : "I understand your anxiety. And I want to help. Not only because he is your father but because there are other people too, in touch with me, who are interested in the Kessel case.

"It occurred to me that you might—even without knowing it—have information which would help, both in the search for Kessel and at the same time to find out where your father is. I think the two things go together."

So the real point was to get information from her. But why not?

She asked : "Don't you think that by interfering you may make difficulties for my father? Wouldn't it be better to let him look after his own affairs. You might upset his own plans."

Dietrich looked as though he were reluctant to say what he thought. Finally he said : "Miss Viner, I don't want to alarm you, but has it not crossed your mind that your father may be held somewhere against his wishes. It is something you must take into account."

"Of course, I have thought of that," Mary said. "But do you know any such thing? Why are you here? Is it blackmail? Can't you, for God's sake, say something definite?"

He ignored the outburst and sat looking at his nails.

"I want to help, Miss Viner," he said quietly.

"I'm sorry. Go on."

"We both went to Amberg, near Nuremberg. Your father was making some inquiries I don't know about and he asked me to try to trace anything about Kessel in the city records. It came to nothing—my work, I mean.

"We were living in a hotel in Nuremberg which happened to be in sight of the Post Office. After supper I would take a stroll or sometimes sit at my window and watch the street. The point is that your father often used to post letters and I noticed that he always put them in the box for letters going abroad. I now wonder whether he was maybe writing to you or to some associate to say what he was doing. He might have written something which would now provide a clue to his whereabouts, or his future plans."

Mary shook her head.

"Perhaps he was writing to a woman friend?"

She shook her head again.

"In any case, it is possible that those letters have a bearing. Did he write much to you?"

"I had only one letter from Nuremberg," Mary said. "It was as usual, a short chatty note. He is not much of a letter-writer. Maybe he was not writing abroad."

Dietrich insisted that he was: "He used airmail envelopes and only bought 50 pfennig stamps. Of course, not necessarily to England. You cannot imagine to whom?"

"No."

"You see, I feel that these letters are important. It is possible that he mentioned the name of the man he was looking for—I mean the name under which Kessel is now going, if we assume that he really still is alive."

Mary went to the writing bureau and pulled down the flap.

"These are all the letters that my father wrote to me from Germany. If there is anything between the lines it certainly escaped me. You are welcome to read them."

She handed him the thin bundle and he read them all very carefully.

"Nothing," he sighed.

He looked at a gold braceleted watch. "If anything new turns up I will tell you at once. I hope I may expect the same from you."

He gave her a card with his name and a West Berlin post office box.

"I move round a lot," he explained.

He had one foot outside the door when he asked: "Did Mr. Blake find out anything useful in East Berlin?" His eyes were simple and clear.

After a moment's pause, Mary said: "Why should you imagine that he went to East Berlin?"

"I was sufficiently interested to find out that he did go over."

"He found out nothing that you seem not to know."

Dietrich put his hand out in the time-honoured Continental way. She took it.

"Good night."

"Good night."

She shut the door and ran up the stairs. She felt as though she had been treated as stupid little girl.

Mary picked her way between the puddles swinging her carrier bag in which she had all the remaining ingredients to make *chilli con carne*. Steve was a terrible man to cook for because he knew too much about it.

Tonight she would outflank him. The *chilli con carne* would be ready and the pancake mix, taking the place of *tortillas*, which not even Steve could make, would be mixed and ready to fry on the table. She had got some lovely rough red wine and there was plenty of time to make a salad—an Indian sambal.

She turned into the front garden, opened the front door and stopped with a gasp. There was someone in the house. Leaving the key in the lock she went silently back to the pavement. The house was in darkness and the certains were open. She had seen nothing and heard nothing that accounted for her feeling.

Within sight of her door were two telephone boxes, back to back. The one nearest the house was occupied, so she waited, not wanting to lose sight of the open front door.

She dialled the *Daily Success* and asked for Steve.

"Darling," she gasped without preamble, "there's someone in the house."

"Do you mean your old man is back?"

"No. it can't be that. There are no lights on and when I opened the door I just felt sure that there was someone there."

"Just a moment," Steve said.

She heard him shouting to someone: "Grab the next two takes off my desk. There's only another stick to come."

"The edition's just going, darling," he said to her. "Make it snappy. Are you sure?"

"Steve, I'm just positive someone is there. I'm scared to go in. I'm in the phone box over the road. I left the door open and ran."

"I'm coming," Steve shouted.

"No, I wasn't talking to you, darling. The edition's going. I can leave in ten minutes but it will take me half an hour to get there."

"What shall I do?"

He groaned. "Get a copper."

"But I don't want to leave the house."

A voice came from the background: "Steve. I've got to have that last copy. We'll be over the top. Chat your bird up later."

"Listen, Mary. Dial 999 and tell them all about it. Wait till a copper comes. I'll be with you in less than an hour."

Directed by their little radios, two foot constables appeared magically at Mary's phone box. One of them waited at the open front door while she led the other down a little side passage to the back garden and up to the back door. Her policeman whispered into his radio and a few seconds later the other policeman opened the back door, from inside.

This one said: "I've slid the bolts on the front door. If there's anyone inside now, it's windows. Can we have some light, miss."

The two men looked into the living-room and kitchen and the cupboard under the stairs.

"That the lot down here?" the senior one asked. "Got a basement, I see. Any way in and out of it?"

"Two windows with bars across."

He slid the bolts on the cellar door, locking it.

"Let's have a butcher's upstairs first."

Nobody upstairs. Nobody in the basement.

"Did you see anyone?" the senior man asked, taking out a notebook and a transparent ballpoint.

"No."

"What gave you the impression that someone was here?"

"I can't really explain it. It was a feeling."

The senior looked at the other policeman, making it clear that in his view this was probably another one of those.

"Got any enemies, miss? Had a row with the boy friend? Any reason to think anyone might want to harm you?"

Mary hesitated. There was no way she could see to explain the whole affair of her father to these two unreceptive types. She shook her head.

"Better take a look round with you and see if anything is missing."

From top to bottom, as far as Mary could tell nothing was missing and nothing was disturbed. And yet everything seemed to have been disturbed, moved, nothing you could put a name to. Her clothes were not quite as she would have left them. Someone had examined the books, pictures, spices in the kitchen, the deep-freeze section of the fridge.

She started to apologize for troubling the police.

"Better be safe than sorry, miss. We'll be getting along. Your imagination plays you tricks sometimes. It's what we're here for, to protect the public. "

FOUR

BLUE TATTOO

I T was still dark when Steve left the next morning for Plymouth where a new grisly murder with cannibalistic overtones had been discovered the previous day.

Mary shut the door after him and picked up the post. When she saw the Berlin postmark she opened the door again but Steve was out of sight.

The letter was on printed notepaper of the Committee of Anti-Fascist Resistance Fighters, Unter den Linden, East Berlin.

"Dear Miss Viner," it began, and went on in school English: "I have allowed myself to write to you personally because I believe we have information about your father which it will be necessary to discuss with you personally. I do not know your financial situation but believing it to be necessary for you to visit us here, I have taken the little liberty of sending you a ticket. We shall also be responsible for your accommodation while you are here. I do assure you that it is in our mutual interest for you to make the journey. You should telephone on arrival. With anti-fascist greeting, Uwe Bergmann."

With the letter was a long blue Interflug ticket: London-Berlin, Schoenefeld-London, made out to Miss Viner.

She looked at the clock. There was no hope of catching Steve now.

Information at Heathrow told her that a Polish LOT plane

was scheduled to leave at 2.50 in the afternoon, direct to Schoenefeld, where it would arrive at 5 p.m. A seat had come vacant last night. She booked it.

If only Steve were here. . . . It might be a trap to get her to East Germany. But would they have sent a letter then? Her name would be on the passenger list, too.

International Exchange told her : of course it was possible to phone East Berlin. She booked a personal call to Herr Uwe Bergmann, and was dressed and waiting when it came. He spoke German only. She would come? Good. At 5 this afternoon a car would be waiting at the airport. No, he was sorry, there was nothing he could say on the telephone.

Something was moving, at any rate. Information concerning her father. What could it be?

There would be the devil to pay with the women's editor. Just back and now off again. Helen, case hardened and ambitious, would scarcely be pleased.

But even if it meant the job itself, she couldn't *not* go now. She packed a little bag and got her passport out.

At the office Helen was fortunately in conference and she left her a humbly apologetic note. Then she wrote a note to Steve. Struck by another idea, she Xeroxed the letter from Bergmann, put the original in the letter to Steve and took a long and expensive detour by taxi to leave it on the table in Steve's flat.

At Schoenefeld airport a plump little man with a big smile introduced himself as Konrad Bieg and whipped her through the customs and passport control leaving the rest of the arrivals in queues. I'm a VIP Mary thought, getting into the black Tatra and returning the driver's *"Guten Abend."*

Herr Bieg showed her to a modern room in the Unter den Linden Hotel. There was a shop in the foyer selling foreign goods, including Scotch and cigarettes and in a lounge was a bar where she had a big gin and tonic. Nothing she had seen conformed to all she had read about the grim drab appearance and life in East Berlin. She had a steak, done very rare and found the service good.

In the foyer, on her way out, a man stood up from an armchair and asked if she was Fraulein Viner.

"Bergmann," he said. He had a long nose with a blue scar above it, deep set eyes, very lively and young, in contrast to a wrinkled, parchment skin. He must have been every bit of sixty but his hair was black, thick and springy. A man and a woman came to them.

"Dr. Ginglass. Frau Fiebig."

Ginglass, the man whom Steve had seen. He was short, plump and bespectacled. She put him down for thirty-five.

"Dr. Ginglass is from the office of the Public Prosecutor," Bergmann said. "We did not know whether you spoke enough German so we brought Frau Fiebig too."

Dr. Ginglass hesitated and said : "We could ask for a conference room or we could go to your room. A conference room is rather formal."

It was a broad hint and Mary said her room. Frau Fiebig went to order coffee and drinks.

As soon as they were sitting in her room Mary asked : "Why is the Public Prosecutor involved? Has my father been arrested?"

A look passed between the two men and the lawyer said : "Nothing like that, Fraulein Viner. In the first place, the Prosecutor was involved because that is the office which deals with investigating cases involving Nazi crimes and war crimes. Now there are other possible reasons."

As he stopped, Mary broke in. "Can't you see that I'm worried about him? Why did you get me to come here? What do you have to tell me—this 'information'?"

"It may not be information at all. That is why we asked you to come. If we had proper contact with the British authorities there would have been no need to waste your time—as I hope, in fact, we are doing."

Mary caught the undercurrent and went quiet.

Ginglass took over.

"Does your father still have the blue tattooed concentration camp number on the left forearm?"

"Yes," Mary said. She added: "He says it is a sort of honour though my mother had hers cut out."

Ginglass took a breath and asked: "Does he have a small piece of shrapnel lodged near the lung under the left arm?"

Fear was growing on Mary's face as she looked at him and grasped slowly the import of his question.

"How can you know? Come, where is my father?"

Bergmann leaned forward.

"I'm afraid we may have bad news for you, Fraulein Viner."

She sat quite still and the lengthening silence grew into only one possibility and then a certainty as neither man spoke.

She whispered: "My father is dead?"

Bergmann nodded, shading his eyes with a parchment hand.

"We think it must be your father."

"Where is he? What happened? Have you. . . ?"

"He was murdered. He—his body—is in East Berlin. We don't know yet what happened."

The body had been reported by Wolfram Ackermann, twenty and Anna Kaul, nineteen, who had not actually seen it but was with Ackermann. It had been hidden in a bunker one kilometre north of Krumme Lake, a nature reserve area.

Cause of death: a heavy blow, probably with a spanner, behind the left ear. A stab wound through the heart had been inflicted after death, no doubt to ensure that death had taken place.

Identification: Considerable effort had been expended to remove every mark of identification.

Face: Beaten to pulp. False teeth removed and several real teeth extracted after death.

Hair: Shaved after death.

Hands: Removed with a sharp blade at wrist joints.

Height: 175 centimetres.

Age: 50 to 60.

Other remarks: A piece of skin has been removed from the left forearm. This might be to create the impression that the dead man had been an inmate in a concentration camp, or it might be to remove the usual tattoo of such inmates.

Date of death: Between October 3 and 18 nearest that pathologists willing to estimate.

Place where body found: Very deserted. A sand road, suitable for cars, runs about two hundred metres from the bunker. This is rarely used in winter since it serves only a small group of cottages on the edge of Muggelspree and Muggelsee. Even one reasonably strong man would not find it hard to carry the body through the woods from the road to the bunker.

Mary turned over the pages of the pathological reports with their gruesome detail.

There was an X-ray photograph of the bomb splinter, other photos in a separate envelope which Ginglass quietly extracted before she had a chance to open it, reports from hospitals: no similar record, police reports: nothing, nothing, nothing.

With memories of the Maria Hagl[1] case, the West German and West Berlin police had been informed. No result so far.

Mary laid the file down and went on staring at the cover, which bore only a number.

Frau Fiebig had gone. The two men sat silently smoking and waiting.

A tough case. One false move and there would be a lovely old hullaballoo in the Western press and radio. "Briton Murdered in East Berlin." "Was Viner Working for the Communists?" Some of his colleagues had opposed Ginglass when he said that Mary must be informed. The man was dead and the murder would certainly be blamed on the East Germans. Better hush the whole thing up.

Ginglass realized that in informing Mary he was risking his job. But he saw her now as the only line leading to Kessel and he wanted Kessel. If she reacted stupidly, if she thought, as she well might, that since her father was murdered in East Berlin, he had been murdered by the "East Germans", it would all be up. Everything now depended on keeping the thing quiet while enquiries still went on with Kessel no doubt sure now that he had closed the doors.

Mary seemed competent and mature. They waited for her to talk—to expose what was in her mind.

At last she said : "I have a request."

"Please."

[1] Maria Hagl, a hotel chambermaid from Frankfurt-on-Main, West Germany was murdered near the Leipzig autobahn in East Germany in December 1966. Her idenity papers were used to smuggle another girl Elke Kempf into West Germany. Maria's lover worked for the Bundesnachrichtendienst (West Germany Secret Service) and owing to her knowledge of this she became a danger to him when they quarrelled. He hit on the plan of driving her into East Germany, murdering her there and taking Elke Kempf back into West Germany in her place.

"I would like to visit the . . . my father. Not to see him. Just to be in the same room for a few minutes."

Ginglass bowed.

They went on waiting.

"One thing : if he was killed here," she said, "your records must be inaccurate. He did cross the border back here, after all."

Ginglass shook his head definitely.

"You may be sure that if your father had come back a third time, the records would show it. It did not happen like that."

"Then how. . . . You say he came and went. He didn't come back but he was killed here. I don't understand what you are trying to say."

"Let me tell you what I think happened; point by point. Your father was absolutely convinced that Kessel is still alive and in Germany. He is living under another name and has almost certainly changed his appearance. I had the most definite impression that Herr Viner knew both his new identity and where he is now."

"But if he knew, what was to stop him simply announcing the fact?"

Ginglass shook his head.

"I think that Herr Viner was more familiar with the German situation than you. In these days, evidence that a man was a Nazi criminal is not enough to bring him to justice, or even to make difficulties for him. In our opinion, Herr Viner wanted to make absolutely sure of getting him, here."

He held up a hand with the fingers spread and then balled them into a fist.

"If your father was getting close, he was a danger to Kessel, but Kessel was a greater danger to him and he knew it. So he wanted to make an 'English departure'. We helped him to make the arrangements for that.

"There is not the least doubt that Herr Viner came here only on October 9 and 11. I have no idea why he came on the ninth.

"When he came on the eleventh, we got his ticket for London and he registered in the Johannishof Hotel. I have had the whole period carefully checked. At about six-fifteen Herr Viner was having a bottle of beer in the lounge when a telephone call came for him.

"According to the receptionist, Herr Viner took the call in one of the cabins in the entrance and left the door ajar.

"Herr Viner spoke for a few moments. She heard him say: 'Are you speaking for Dr. Ginglass?' She recalled the name because it had been my secretary who had booked the room and she was to send the bill to my office.

"Then Herr Viner said something about being ready in ten minutes. He went back and finished his beer, got his coat and went out. He did not return."

He paused to let that register and went on: "It is sure that Herr Viner was somehow decoyed out of the Johannishof. Certainly nobody made a call from my office. He was murdered that evening and somebody else went out, back to West Berlin, using Herr Viner's passport."

"But," Mary interrupted.

He held up a plump hand.

"One moment please. The people we are dealing with have all the resources. They could have a man here, smuggled or on false papers, sufficiently resembling your father to have passed back through the border as him. And so, Herr Viner seemed to have entered East Berlin and returned. They even telephoned Herr Viner's pension and had his bag collected. Very tidy. It should have been the perfect murder."

Bergman leaned forward. "If Herr Blake had not come to see Dr. Ginglass, we would never have connected the body found in the woods at Muggelsee with Herr Viner at all."

Mary passed a limp hand over her forehead.

"It is hard for me to understand the importance of these details. Why did someone have to go back to West Berlin with my father's passport? If my father was killed and unidentifiable, nothing more needed to be done."

At this question Ginglass looking like a triumphant counsel who has skilfully led a witness into a pitfall.

"You see, Fraulein Viner, that is the whole matter. Unless someone went back using your father's passport, our border records would show that a certain Herr Viner entered but did not leave. This was exactly what the murderers wanted to avoid. They needed our records to show that Herr Viner came and went. Thus it would not be possible for anyone to connect him with the body. He would be presumed to have disappeared—anywhere but here."

"I see that," Mary said. "But . . . never mind."

"I think I see what is on your mind. You are understandably suspicious of everyone, ourselves included," Bergmann said. "The possibility remains that we could have sent someone over the border, using Herr Viner's passport: one, to make it appear that he had returned to West Berlin and, two, to pick up his suitcase with anything we might have wanted from it."

Mary met his eyes. He had judged exactly what she was thinking.

"It is possible," she said.

"Entirely," Bergman said. "But why should we go to such pains to commit a perfect, undetectable murder and then inform you about it?"

"I suppose," Mary said miserably, "that if my father were

a spy, you might still think that I might know something or that you might find out something through me."

"But then," Ginglass said, "if we had your father in our hands, why should we kill him and go through the rest of these manoeuvres? Killing spies is old-fashioned. It is better to keep them alive."

He added hastily: "Miss Viner, forgive me if I seem callous. We are most anxious that you should have confidence in us."

Bergmann said: "I think we can leave Fraulein Viner to work all that out for herself. She evidently has a good grasp of the problem."

Ginglass nodded. He tapped the file. "You can judge from this, Fraulein Viner," he said, "that it is not even going to be easy to prove that your father has been murdered. The only evidence of identity is—or might be—that X-ray of the shrapnel shard. Your father was a military man and therefore it is possible that the army, rather the air force, has an X-ray photo taken at the time which would serve for identification. Or maybe a hospital which he attended later. Owing to the lack of diplomatic relations with Great Britain, your help in this matter could be of great value."

"I shall do all that I can." She sounded weary and without spirit.

Ginglass went on: "Since the murderer or murderers came from West Berlin, our enquiries are handicapped. We shall do what we can. But it may be possible that in your fathers' papers in London, he may have left a note or something. He may have actually indicated what lines of inquiry he was pursuing or even the name of the man who is actually Kessel."

Dietrich! Mary's hands stiffened on the arms of her chair. Should she tell them? No. First talk it over with Steve. She had made enough mistakes.

She said: "I will see if there is anything in London that will help."

Bergmann intervened.

"Dr. Ginglass, I think we should let Fraulein Viner get some sleep. She has had a terrible shock and we cannot expect her to be able to think clearly and discuss."

Mary looked at her watch. It was ten o'clock. Impossible to believe that she had been in London this morning. But she knew she would not be able to sleep. She said so.

Bergmann looked across at Ginglass. "I think it would be a good idea if I were to take Fraulein Viner over the road to the Linden Corso for a bottle of wine. I could tell you about your father when I knew him."

"You knew him?"

"Yes. I knew him very well. I was also in Sachsenhausen, you see."

The lawyer said: "Uwe spent 12 years in prisons and camps. A veteran. In 1945 he saved your father's life."

FIVE

KESSEL'S FINGERPRINTS

THERE was no moon. Harold Viner felt the tug of the harness as his parachute opened and watched the bomber that had brought him from England burst into flame and light up the countryside in a blaze of disintegration. Floating down among bursts of flak, he could see flashes in Berlin as the bombs went down. A searchlight blinded him, then held him as he swung down. Others rotated to join it, bathing him in light. He could see no other 'chutes.

He landed badly in the dark, slipping the parachute by reflex. Then he was lying half-conscious with frozen snow pricking his face. There was a lot to be done according to training—'chute gathered up and hidden; a route worked out to escape.

As he stood up headlights came blazing round a bend. Then he was running—fast as the heavy gear let him. A gloved fist broke the night into flashes and as he hit the ground a boot crashed into his ribs. More boots and, as he writhed, a gun butt swung between his legs and brought a scream of pain. But they had not killed him. He was gun-barrelled along the icy road in the wake of the long-disappeared jeep.

They came to a long grey wall lit up from behind. From watchtowers at intervals, curious guards peered down at the little group and one of his captors shouted up: "Englander." He slipped on the crystalline road and everyone laughed.

"Get up, pig," someone called and they laughed again. The notice said :

Area Headquarters
Sachsenhausen Preventive Detention Camp
KEEP OUT
Trespassers Will Be Shot Without
Warning !

Newly captured British airmen did not arrive every day at Sachsenhausen, though there were a dozen or more British war prisoners in the Special Camp outside the main camp. These had been sent from other camps.

Viner was ordered to be placed in the cell block, the solitary confinement block inside the main camp. In fact it was a prison within a prison, under the charge of Hauptscharfuehrer[1] Eccarius. He was to be kept isolated during his period of military interrogation and then handed over to the camp authorities.

Of all the SS officers in Sachsenhausen, the one most feared by the underground leaders of the prisoners was Hauptsturmfuehrer[2] Wolfgang Kessel. Slender, foppish and vain, he had nonetheless a shrewd brain and the ability to find the weakness of others and use them for his own ends.

It had been Kessel who had succeeded in uncovering a group of the leaders of the camp resistance movement by observation and judicious application of torture. This had looked as though it would uncover the entire secret leadership which had been built up over years until a key member of the Komitee had succeeded in dying under Eccarius' treatment without betraying his next contacts.

Kessel himself never watched nor took part in the maltreat-

[1] Hauptscharfuehrer: SS rank approximating to sergeant-major. Eccarius was sentenced to life at hard labour after the war.
[2] Hauptsturmfuehrer: SS rank approximating to Captain.

ment of the prisoners by the other SS guards. Nor was he popular with them for he did not bother to hide the contempt he evidently had for their coarseness and brutality. His pleasure lay in the evocation of fear; in raising hope and dashing it to despair, leaving others to carry out the practical bestialities involved.

Viner was called to his office on a cold morning. He stood at attention, cap in hand, waiting to be addressed.

Kessel wore his uniform with ease and moved with careful grace. He had an extremely high narrow nose, like a hawk's beak, which was noticeably bent to the left. It was out of character with his full, almost feminine lips, blue eyes with long lashes and smooth cheeks shaved and powdered to perfection. He had long ear lobes and wore his blond hair cut very close at the sides.

He greeted Viner with a friendly nod and offered him a cigarette, his first since his interrogation by the Luftwaffe. He lit his own and pushed the matches across the table to enable Viner to do the same. There was also something feminine in the way he smoked, holding the cigarette between his right thumb and forefinger and constantly giving it little flicks with his fourth finger.

His English accent fascinated Viner. Grammatically he was fairly good but his pronunciation was of the "hard" German kind and his vowels took Viner some time to place. Then he realized that Kessel must have learned English either from a Scotsman or from a German who had learned it in Scotland or from a Scotsman. There was no mistaking it once he had traced it to its source and he listened for each additional proof.

When he said that he feared Viner's stay in Sachsenhausen might be a "wee bit irksome", the matter was settled. Here was a German talking Scottish with a German accent.

Kessel hoped that it might not be for too long. Wars did

not last for ever. Viner would realize that as in England, times were hard, he said, commiserating with Viner on the poor quality of the thin, blue and white striped ticking uniform and the wood-soled clogs.

Der Fuehrer, he remarked, was absolutely furious over the allied bombing raids on Berlin—and had ordered captured allied flyers to be kept in rigorous conditions. He hoped that Viner did not feel the cold. It was time he became acquainted at first hand with the ways of the camp. A batch of new arrivals was on its way and he would have an opportunity to see them inducted.

Viner asked when he would be put with the other British war prisoners.

Kessel raised an eyebrow and said, deprecatingly, that the authorities understood that he was a Jew. Jews were not allowed to be kept with Gentiles. For the time being he must remain in the cell block. And wear the yellow triangle.[1]

Viner was marched out to stand in the thin driving snow at one corner of the semicircular mustering ground. In ten minutes he was shuddering with cold. He was not permitted to warm himself by clapping his arms or stamping. Two hours later the new arrivals filed raggedly through the main gates and shuffled into lines, to wait.

Another hour passed in the wind and a fine snow covered the shivering newcomers. Then there was a stir and round the corner came three SS men, woollen greatcoats reaching below their knee-high boots, belt buckles shining. They were block leaders—"Iron" Gustav Sorge, Wilhelm Schubert and Fritz Ficker.[2]

---

[1] Concentration camp inmates could be distinguished at a glance by the colour of the cloth triangle sewn over their hearts, Red—political; Yellow—Jew; Blue—Stateless; Green—Criminal; Pink—Homosexual.
[2] All three were later sentenced to life at hard labour by a military court.

They stopped by the first man in the front row.

"Why are you here?" Sorge asked.

The other two block leaders waited, smiling in anticipation.

The man mumbled that he was a "political".

Sorge's heavily gloved fist took him in the mouth and nose. Blood poured and he attempted to wipe it away.

Sorge bellowed. "Answer me before you wipe that pig's blood from your snout."

"I was denounced. I don't know who did it."

"Ha! An innocent angel. What party?"

"Social Democrat."

Sorge's fist drove him back into the row behind and then a kick in the belly dropped him to the ground.

Ficker stopped in front of an old man.

"Why aren't you standing at attention?"

"Mister, let me go to the lavatory. I've got chronic stomach trouble. My guts are falling out."

Ficker shouted at him: "What will these dogs want next?"

He put his right hand over his left shoulder to give the old man a backhander but just then Sorge shouted:

"Lie down."

They lay at full length in the snow.

"There's the intake barrack. Now roll to it."

Helped by kicks, the whole prone ranks rolled in the snow all the way to the barrack entrance. One stayed still, giving no response to the kicks and they left him lying, snow gradually covering him. It was the old man with stomach trouble.

When they had gone inside, Viner's guard gave him a nudge with his gun muzzle and jerked his head toward the cell block.

"Your father was a very good man," Bergmann said. "He suffered very much."

"And finally they killed him."

Bergmann patted her hand. He poured some more wine from their second bottle.

"He never told you about Kessel?"

"Not in detail. Only how much he hated him," Mary said.

Bergmann nodded. "Kessel was a pervert. He got his greatest pleasure by raising hope and then dashing hope into despair. He loved to see fear in the eyes of others. Of course, only if he had arranged the circumstances.

"He made a special victim of your father, because he was Jewish, I suppose. For example, he would arrange that your father would be made to watch a man hanging with his arms behind him from his wrists until he had fainted and been brought round several times, screaming and out of his senses with pain. Then he sent for your father, gave him a cigarette, even a drink, chatted about the war, raised his hopes that maybe at last he would get the treatment of a war prisoner. At a suitable moment, a lower officer would come in and announce that your father had been sentenced to hang by his wrists on the next day. By the time that had been repeated several times—Kessel always polite, correct and apparently commiserating, there was a definite relationship established. It is easy to understand that your father would never want to talk about such humiliation. However unwillingly, he was participating with Kessel in Kessel's perversions. And, of course, he was totally alone, without the benefit of organization, which we had."

Bergmann finished the wine in his glass and poured more for both.

"There is no need for me to say any more about that. It is enough for you to understand that your father would go to any lengths to see that Kessel paid some price for his crimes. I, too, even though it might be for different reasons."

"Dr. Ginglass said you saved his life," Mary said.

"I and others. I didn't even know him and what I did was done for mixed reasons. You must understand that by that time everyone realized that the Nazis were on the run from the Russian army and the SS in Sachsenhausen and other camps were speeding up the killing of the camp inmates. One day they murdered most of the war prisoners, mostly Russians but also including seven British prisoners.

"Your father escaped this massacre because he was in the cell block in solitary confinement. You probably don't know much about the camps."

Mary shook her head.

"Well, you must realize that running a large camp like that needed a great deal of organization. The SS was too lazy, incompetent and arrogant to do it. They passed over most of the work to the prisoners. The result was that we 'politicals' took it over and slowly built up a secret organization.

"In the end practically every block senior and his assistant as well as everyone working in the clothing and food stores, office and infirmary and so on, was appointed by the underground committee.

"The real problem was protecting the heart of organization —the committee itself. Committee members rarely took any official position in the administration. We took only lowly, inconspicuous tasks and our identity was not known even by members of the organization living in their own blocks."

"And you," Mary asked. "What were you doing?"

"I was for the last period, chairman of the committee. I had been by that time twelve years inside, having been formerly a Communist town councillor. Luckily I had been a watchmaker. It made a superb cover. My SS block leader was a brainless idiot who would never have survived a day without a capable prisoner-clerk. I was that clerk. But clerks were ten a penny. Watchmakers were another story.

"In wartime there are always shortages and soon everyone in the SS at the camp was taking watches to my SS block leader to be repaired. He charged high prices and naturally paid me nothing. But his ability to remain more or less permanently drunk rested on my watchmaking skill. He would have protected me in any circumstances. And not even the prisoner block-senior in my barrack knew that I was a member of the committee which had secretly appointed him.

"At that time we were preparing for an armed uprising. It was clear that the SS would not retreat without trying to wipe out everyone in the camp. The problem was not to act too early or too late.

"Kessel went away to some SS meeting at the time and your father became so ill that he looked like dying. He was in a raging fever. Eccarius, the boss of the cell block and one of the worst Nazis in the camp was so worried that it was clear he had orders to keep your father alive.

"Eccarius sent for the infirmary senior, a prisoner named Jockel, one of our men. He told Jockel to take your father to the infirmary and treat him. 'I want him back alive for Kessel,' Eccarius said. 'No tricks. If he dies, I shall want the body.' This was because we used to switch bodies as a way of changing people's identities.

"That night Jockel sent a report to the committee and we learned that the last remaining British prisoner—a Jew at that—was in the infirmary.

"We had a hot discussion over what to do. From the first I was in favour of making your father 'disappear'.

"I argued that we needed to take some initiative and test the degree of SS nervousness. Camp morale was declining. The inmates feared a massacre. If morale declined, so would organization. I took the view that Kessel was a kind of lone wolf and not liked by the other SS officers who would be happy to see him discomfited. They might make a perfunctory search and fail and that would raise morale. Others argued that it was folly to risk a camp search over one man. But he was the only surviving Western prisoner and also a Jew. It was plainly our duty as well to save him.

"To keep it short, that was the decision. Your father and Jockel disappeared. We hid them in a cave built under a pile of coal in the cookhouse."

"And what happened?"

"Nothing at all. We had to take other steps to gain the initiative. When Kessel came back there was too much chaos for him to get anywhere about the case of a single captured airman."

Bergmann took Mary to the airport. The plane was late but coffee and cognac came.

"Why did your father come to Germany?" Bergmann said. "Not to pursue Kessel?"

"He thought Kessel was dead. He saw his blood-stained identity papers. He married a German girl, you know," Mary said.

"I know. Her name was. . . . It began with M."

"Marcuse."

"Ruth Marcuse."

"You knew her?"

"She was also rescued by the camp committee. Sometimes it was possible. She was very beautiful, as I recall."

Mary spun her cognac glass and put it down again, before she said: "Mother died in 1965. Soon after, my father got £2,000 compensation for having been held in Sachsenhausen. There was a struggle with the Foreign Office in London but in the end they had to pay. So there was Dad, single, no rent to pay, with £2,000 to spend. I persuaded him to take a long holiday, travelling round and enjoying himself. He wanted me to go with him but I had just got a very good job and it would have been foolish to leave it. So off he went by himself.

"I was surprised to find that he had gone to Germany. I would have thought that he would want to forget it. But I suppose it was a nostalgic longing to visit old places where he had been with my mother. For a week or two I got long chatty letters from various German towns. Then the letters got few and short. It seemed to me a good sign that he was forgetting the past and beginning to take an interest in the present."

A click and a hum warned that the loudspeakers were live.

"Passengers for the LOT Flight 239 please get ready to embark," they said in four languages.

There was a bustle among the waiting guests and Dr. Ginglass came hurrying busily through saying how glad he was that the plane was late.

"I called your office," he said to Bergmann, "and they told me you had gone, and so my secretary called the airport and they told her that the plane was delayed by weather so I decided to come out. I was lucky, I see."

Mary watched Bergmann sigh inaudibly.

"Passengers for LOT Flight 239 for London, please go immediately to the embarkation exits. Have your boarding cards ready, please."

"Just in time," Ginglass said.

"Well?" Bergmann asked.

"Yes." Ginglass dived into his portfolio and his hand came out with some photostats.

"Kessel's fingerprints," he said triumphantly.

Mary picked up one of the copies. The fingerprints of the man who had tortured her father. They were in two rows, sharp and clear, Xeroxed from an old police record printed in Gothic type and with the entries obviously written with a steel nib. The date was 1931 and the name was Wolfgang Kessel, date of birth, March 26, 1913.

"Sentenced to one year with several other youths for a sexual assault on a young woman. He got a light sentence because he had not participated in the sexual assault but had been present and was therefore an accomplice."

"Typical," Bergman said dryly.

Ginglass gathered up the prints.

All the other passengers had gone and the stewardess was looking impatient.

"Take these," he said. "I have others."

Mary put them in her bag.

"I will tell you if I can find out anything in London," she said.

SIX

SCOTTISH ACCENT

MR. MICHAEL GOLDFIELD of Goldfield, Goldfield, Beddow and Turner, solicitors, looked over the flat tops of his tiny semicircular reading glasses and solemnly stated that it was a most unusual case.

"I must confess," he said, "that we have never undertaken a case which concerned East Germany and so I shall be impelled to examine the legal aspects of the matter."

It was disconcerting, Mary found, to be examined by rather bulgy eyes from between bushy eyebrows and the straight-edged top of the glasses.

"We shall find very little in precedent to help us, I fear. Without an X-ray photo which can be specifically identified as one of your father's I fail, on the basis of what you have said, to see how it will be possible to identify the deceased as your father or—which would naturally be the desirable alternative—to exclude that possibility."

God preserve me, Mary thought and said: "It's not really surprising. It was war time. The shrapnel never caused him any trouble. Even his own doctor didn't know it was there."

He nodded and tapped soft, pink, beautifully manicured fingertips together. "Without such identification and bearing in mind what you have told me of the care taken to remove all signs of identity, I would say, without prejudice, that the authorities in East Germany can hardly treat the matter as anything but the murder of an unidentifiable person. Certainly no British court would accept that he was your father. Moreover, you did not see the remains. Great pity."

"What on earth difference would it make?"

He coughed. "In the circumstances, a statement from you that you had seen the remains and were satisfied that the deceased was Harold Viner—regardless of the actual situation —would carry weight in an English court."

"I would sooner remember my father as he was."

"Most understandable." He sighed. "But it alters the situation. I am really in a quandary, Miss Viner.

"I told you on the telephone that a number of letters had come in the past weeks from Germany, in Mr. Viner's handwriting and addressed: To be collected by the addressee. I regret that I told you that. It was a breach of professional confidence. To allow you to read them is out of the question."

Exasperation broke through. "But I am his daughter—his only relative. And I am sure he is dead. That shrapnel. . . ."

He put his fingertips together. "It could be a coincidence or a trick. Anyone who knew about it or had an old X-ray photo of your father could reproduce such an X-ray photo without trouble, from a living or a dead person. In an X-ray photograph it may not be possible to tell whether a bit of metal is lying on a person's chest, between his back and the bed or embedded in the flesh."

"You mean he may still be alive?"

"I wish I could believe it for your sake, but as a lawyer speculation does not interest me. We require evidence. There is no evidence, available to me or to an English court, that he is dead. That being so the matter must rest until such time as he can legally be presumed dead. Then there are the political problems. I have not yet studied the detailed legal matters involved but what I know about East Germany is only that legally it does not exist."

"Well, I've been there," Mary snorted. "It exists, I can assure you."

"But not so far as we are concerned."

"But apart from the law," Mary said impatiently. "Those letters may shed some light on a crime."

"Apart from the law! My dear Miss Viner! Suppose your father were to appear tomorrow and find that I have handed his private letters to you. What then? I am responsible in law."

"But I am his daughter."

The lawyer made a gesture of patience strained beyond limit. "Relationships between members of families may be excellent but they may also be hostile and frequently are. I cannot be judge of such matters. I can do only what the law allows."

"Were there many letters?" Mary asked desperately.

"Several, I think. My clerk brought the first one to me and I instructed him to put it in Mr. Viner's deed box. He later mentioned that there were others."

"Were they in my father's handwriting?"

"I believe so. I have no objection to their being brought here for you to see. Of course, without due legal permission, they must remain sealed."

Mary nodded. "I would like to see them."

He pressed the intercom and a few moments later a bald sparrow of a man in an ancient suit sidled in. Mr. Goldfield spread the letters along the desk. They were all in similar airmail envelopes, postmarked Munich, Nuremberg, Berlin.

"They are in father's handwriting." Mary looked along the row. Some were thick and some seemed to contain only a single sheet. She looked closer and saw that one in the middle looked different. It had a blurred date stamp and she leaned over to get a closer look. It had been posted on October 11.

Suddenly she said: "Look, this one from East Berlin is addressed to me."

Mr. Goldfield first picked up all the letters and then riffled through them. He looked closer. "Miss Mary Viner. Do not forward."

He looked at the clerk.

"Is anything wrong, sir?"

"My attention should have been drawn to this, Hibble."

"I am sorry, sir. I put it with the others. It said not to be forwarded."

"I should have been informed."

"Very sorry, sir. I. . . ." It was a familiar situation.

"At any rate, Miss Viner, this letter is addressed to you. I did not know of its existence."

Mary ripped it open and read it. With difficulty she suppressed her exultation and tried to kill the air of triumph with which she handed it to Mr. Goldfield. It was very short.

"To Whom it May Concern: I, Harold Viner, hereby empower my daughter, Mary Penelope Viner, to act on my behalf in all my affairs."

It was signed by Harold Viner and two witnesses, both with English addresses. The date was October 10.

Goldfield studied it closely and seemed to get some comfort from the fact that it was in proper legal form.

"It is a Power of Attorney," he said, relishing the words. "I shall need to confirm the witnesses' signatures, of course. But it is apparently in order."

The first letter was thick. Inside was a note on a single sheet of paper.

"My darling Mary,

"I wrote you yesterday that I was going to Berlin. Actually I intended to have a look round old places and maybe even visit Sachsenhausen again. Now something has happened to change my plans. When you read the enclosed notes, you will know why. I am writing it down because, you never know, at my age I might have a heart attack or get killed in an accident. So I hope that you will never read this letter or the notes.

"For the first time since Ruth died I feel I have some reason to live. Revenge, they say, is an ignoble motive. If so, I would prefer to say that I want to see justice done. Justice is a kind of revenge. All my love, Mary. Your Daddy."

The other pages in the letter were in Viner's neat writing and were numbered. The first began without preamble:

"I got a real shock last night. I was in a pub, leaning on the bar and watching the television screen. The news came on and the big item was about a meeting in London between delegations from West Germany, Britain and the Netherlands to settle the details about joint development of the process of producing enriched uranium by the gas centrifuge process. Fools we have always been as far as the Germans are concerned. This would give them the H-Bomb on a silver platter.

"An interviewer came on with a microphone and turned to the leading West German industrialist on the delegation.

"It was a typical sort of technique. The interviewer and the German, whose name I didn't catch, were both speaking English. They started with English and then faded it off into a German translation. But suddenly I felt as though I had woken up in the middle of a dream about falling—a kind of shock to the guts. It was the voice.

"I had heard that voice before, speaking English with just that mixture of a German and Scottish accent. I had very good reason to know that voice. It took a moment but then I was utterly sure. I could not believe my eyes though.

"This was a totally different man—a man with a straight

well-shaped nose, quite different ears, dark hair and eyebrows. I had just decided that coincidences can happen and this one might have learned his English from the same teacher as Kessel when he put a cigarette to his mouth. He had exactly that gesture which Kessel had, holding it between finger and thumb and constantly flicking it with his fourth finger.

"I still couldn't be sure. But after all those years that voice gave me cold shivers. I couldn't sleep for hearing it, very urbane, talking about the glowing prospects of trade and relations within a United States of Europe."

Under the following day's date Viner wrote :

"Of course, when I bought *Die Welt*, there he was and I recognized him as no other than Josef Koll. More need not be said. Josef Koll, the man who has shot into the biggest big business interests, with umpteen interlocking companies and a vast industrial and financial empire with its offices in West Berlin. Next stop : West Berlin."

The next notes were dated two days later :

"I never realized how difficult it is to get close to a really rich man. He has a magnificent house in Grunewald, where I went and waited around from 8 a.m. It's the kind of way out place with a high wall and steel gates operated electrically. Soon after ten the gates slid open and a Bentley sailed out—chauffeur driven—curtained at the back. That was that. I didn't see a thing.

"So I hung round his offices. No Bentley. I sat in a pub to keep out of sight. Soon after one o'clock the Bentley turned up and I went out and grabbed a taxi. Told him to wait and follow the Bentley, feeling a bit like James Bond. The ride took a few moments—to Kempinski's. I didn't dare follow him straight into the restaurant. Sat in the lounge, ordered a drink, pretended to read a paper and after a decent pause I got a table in the restaurant well away from the quarry and observed him. There is not any doubt at all. Josef Koll is Wolfgang Kessel."

At this point Viner seemed to have started a new page, at a later time.

"It was just a bit of sheer luck that I heard Koll speaking English. I would never have recognized him otherwise. But faced with the fact that Koll is Kessel, I find that I simply don't know what to do next.

"One starting point might be to find out whether there was a genuine Josef Koll and what became of him. If Josef Koll ever existed, there must be some record of the fact somewhere on paper, or I don't know the Germans. Germans can't just pop up through the floor without documentary evidence of their existence."

Viner's next letter was from Nuremberg and on the headed notepaper of a pension.

"Long live bureaucracy and German thoroughness. For a mere 100 marks a Bonn private enquiry agent has sifted it out. Josef Koll, now the industrial and financial big-shot, was humbly born on May 5, 1915 and was named Franz-Josef Koll. Very convenient, that. Merely by dropping the Franz, the name has an unfamiliar ring to old intimates. Franz-Josef Koll was born at 23 Waldstrasse, Amberg. His father was Hans Koll, a clerk. His mother was one Ingrid Meyer but there is no information about where she came from. Franz-Josef had one younger sister, Friede. He was inducted into the Wehrmacht and served without distinction until the end of the war.

"But Hans, Ingrid and Friede Koll all met a tragic fate on the night of June 10, 1945. The little house in which they lived and where Franz-Josef had been born, was burned down. Their charred bodies were found in the ashes.

"I found that a small block of new flats stands on the site

of 23 Waldstrasse but over the road the old houses still stood. I knocked at several before I found a neighbour who had known the Kolls—Thomas Reinfahrt. It had been an especially sad affair, he said, because only that day they had had news of their son, Franz-Josef, from the Eastern front. A comrade of his, in civilian clothes, had made a detour to bring them news about Franz-Josef. He was alive and well but would not be able to get back to Amberg for a week or two.

"Frau Koll had at once rushed down the road to tell her friend Frau Reinfahrt. The comrade of Franz-Josef had even brought a present from their son, some sausage and schnapps which they would have for supper because the friend had to be on his way at once, that night. Then in the middle of the night the house had gone up in flames. Everyone thought that the Kolls had probably drunk too much of the wood alcohol that passed as schnapps. There had been no enquiries. War time. Nobody but the Kolls had seen their son's friend.

"Curiously enough, Franz-Josef Koll never turned up either. 'Probably heard what happened and stayed away,' Herr Reinfahrt said.

"Kessel is alive, so he certainly was not killed in the SS staff jeep. However it was arranged, he certainly must have put his own SS papers in the pocket of one of the dead men. What then would be easier than to pick up with a suitable Wehrmacht soldier from among the thousands who were 'demobbing' themselves, murder him and take his papers and maybe his uniform, probably depositing the other SS papers on his body to clinch the matter. He would then be safe. Nobody bothered with low ranking Wehrmacht soldiers.

"His sole danger would be from people who knew Franz-Josef Koll in Amberg, but of those, especially his relatives. Would a man like Kessel cavil at going to Amberg and wiping them out?"

All the other letters detailed Viner's frustrations: his search for another related Koll; the embarrassed refusal of the British Military Mission to help. Was not Koll the man who was going to get Britain into Europe, the new Europe with its own everything including the H-Bomb? Viner recorded his failure to get anywhere with the West Berlin police.

The last letter but one was dated October 9.

"I have been wondering whether I should go over to East Berlin and see if the Communists can do anything. Yesterday I popped over the border, just to look round but I couldn't make my mind up. Then I saw on the S-Bahn map that trains ran to Oranienburg and on the spur of the moment got on one and went to look at Sachsenhausen. They've turned it into a memorial.

"Most of the people there were groups, school outings and people from factories being conducted round. Individual visitors were few. That's why I noticed this chap, dressed in a very German style with a short raglan cut coat, half-belted and a tight-brimmed Robin Hood hat. Then I saw him again at Ostkreuz where I had to change.

"I went through the usual procedure at Friedrichstrasse and found a Wansee train waiting upstairs. I got in but then noticed it was not a smoker. So I got out and ran down to a smoker and darted in as the doors shut. And there was the same man again. A bit too much to be a coincidence."

Viner's last letter addressed to himself was a thick one. It was written on the notepaper of the Ebert Pension and dated October 10.

"Today the balloon went up," it started. "I have to get out of here. That much is clear. What then? I decided that I ought to try out the East German people. After breakfast I walked out toward Kurfürstendamm.

"An Opel Rekord was parked at the kerb in Bleibtreustrasse and as I got level with it, wondering how to make sure I was not being followed, the back door opened and a man leaned forward saying : 'Pardon me, can you tell me. . . .'

"I hardly heard the swish of feet behind me and then the man in the car grabbed my lapels and someone behind pushed and I was sprawling in the back of the car. The door slammed shut and was on the move before I could even sit up. I was pushed down on to the seat by the man who had pulled me in. A man was leaning over the front seat, his arm along it, and then I noticed that he had a small pistol pointing at me from under his arm.

" 'What?' I started to say.

" 'Shut up, Jew pig. And keep still,' he said. I thought he was grinning at first but then I saw it was his normal expression.

" 'Don't make a move'," he said, 'especially at the traffic lights.'

"When we stopped at the lights, people were only a foot or two away but they might have been in the Sahara for all I could do. Nobody said anything more till we got into Grunewald Forest. They pulled up at the side of the road in a large empty space.

" 'Okay, here, Max?' the driver asked.

" 'Okay. See if he's clean,' the man called Max said to the one in the back. He padded me all over, and nodded. I never heard him speak.

"Max told them both to get out of the car. I suppose that when I found myself alone with Max I must have shown that I was looking for some way to get out. He said : 'Don't try anything silly, Jew.'

"What do you want with me? I asked, trying to keep my voice from trembling.

"Max simply lit a cigarette and flicked a switch. He did

both without letting the gun move from me. I heard a faint hum in the car.

" 'Max here,' he said. 'Okay!'

"A tinny voice from a loudspeaker answered at once. 'Is he there? Viner?'

" 'Yes.'

" 'The others?'

" 'Outside.'

" 'Good. You can get outside too. No mistakes. If he tries anything, shoot to kill. Check every five minutes.'

"Max said : 'You heard,' and got out.

"I was alone in the car and I could see them outside, two on the near side and one lounging on the offside.

" 'Viner,' the voice said.

"I answered and he said : 'Someone wants to speak to you.'

"There was a click and the hum changed its note.

" 'Viner.'

"Yes.

" 'Do you know who is speaking?' The voice spoke in English. It was undoubtedly Kessel's voice and accent—German and Scottish.

" 'Yes.'

" 'Pardon me for any inconvenience I have caused you, but. . . .'

" 'Cut the playacting,' I burst out in rage. 'What do you want?'

" 'Let me first tell you the situation.' He spoke German now. 'This radio telephone is scrambled and nobody can pick up this conversation. This is why I chose this method. The men outside the car have no knowledge of what is involved or that they are working for me. The car is untraceable.'

" 'Why don't you get to the point?'

" 'I intend to. You will stop your present investigations; leave Germany and stay out.'

"I didn't answer. For a long time all that could be heard was the hum of the radio telephone.

" 'Well?' he asked.

" 'And if I refuse?' I asked.

" 'It does not arise in that way. You are going to stop your investigations in any case. I am merely giving you a chance— one chance only—to co-operate. Otherwise there will certainly be serious consequences for yourself.'

" 'Magnanimous,' I said, or something like it.

" 'Expedient,' he said. 'I would prefer to be sure that the matter is dropped in such a way that it will not be necessary for enquiries to be made?'

"At that moment the door opened and Max put his head in. 'Reporting,' he said.

" 'Five minutes,' the radio said and Max banged the door shut.

" 'Herr Viner,' the voice went on. 'I know all about your visits to Amberg, the British Mission, the police and so on. Your mistake lay in believing that the German cadre changed after the war. But you will find that everyone wants to forget past follies—our allies no less. Nobody wants these dusty old skeletons got out of long closed cupboards.'

" 'If it's so simple,' I said, 'what is worrying you? Why all this trouble?'

"He did not pause, just went on very self-sure.

" 'Of course I prefer not having a possibility of scandal. Yesterday you crossed to East Berlin. You went and had a look at the Communist headquarters. Then you went to Sachsenhausen. I understand your possible nostalgic desire to re-visit Sachsenhausen. But the visit to the Communist headquarters seems to me to indicate a train of thought.'

"He seemed worried and suddenly I felt a bit more cheerful.

" 'Those people over there never miss a chance to make propaganda against Germany. At the present time I prefer not to be the target of a propaganda campaign. I am at the centre of vital negotiations.

" 'I have to balance the risks. You are after all a British prisoner from Sachsenhausen and that would lend a special twist to the affair. It would be attractive to the press. On the other hand, if you were simply to disappear, that might also lead to problems. Clearly the most satisfactory solution would be for you to drop the whole affair.'

" 'Most of all for you,' I said. 'I have an account to settle with you, Herr Kessel-Koll.'

" 'Not only for me. For you too. I am a very rich man. Name a reasonable sum which would indemnify you for what you consider I owe and it will be transferred to your bank at once. It is a generous offer.'

" 'And if I don't accept it?'

" 'I have already indicated the alternative. I am quite serious. You either accept my offer or you accept the consequences of not doing so. I will make myself clear. I was thinking in terms of, say, up to £20,000.'

" 'It's a lot of money for what you reckon to be nothing,' I said.

" 'It is not nothing,' Kessel said. 'How did you recognize me?'

" 'By your speech.'

" 'Precisely,' he said. 'Only an Englishman could have spotted it and that means yourself, since you were the only one I met till the war was over. I think I have made the situation clear and I have no more time to spend on it. You must leave Berlin by the first plane and at the latest by tomorrow. As soon as you are back in London I will have the money paid into your bank. If you remain, or if you return to Berlin. . . . Well, this is the last warning you will have. That is all.'

"He must have switched over, because the humming changed note and the first voice came on and said: 'Wait for Max, Viner.'

"Max reappeared.

" 'Okay, Max,' the voice said. 'Get the others in and put the Englishman out.'

"The driver started up and Max said: 'Get out Jew'."

The next sheet was dated the same day, October 10, evening.

"Supposing I was being followed, I went to the airline office this afternoon and booked a ticket on a flight to London tomorrow afternoon. I also paid up at the pension till tomorrow morning and told them I would be leaving during the day. It was £25 I hated spending—for the air ticket, I mean—because I have other plans. Still, I suppose I can reclaim it. I intend to drop this letter in the pension post, go out to a meal and a cinema and to bed. Tomorrow morning I shall go out when the morning rush hour traffic is at its best and try to lose my tail, as I believe it is called. I shall cross over to East Berlin and try to get the people there to try to trace Kessel's past. I won't tell them more than necessary in case they spoil the whole thing by some premature leakage. But I simply can't go on like this. I have to have time to think and maybe get a private inquiry agent working for me. Certainly I have no intention of giving up but there is no sense in working the way I have been doing."

SEVEN

SHOWDOWN

WHEN Mary went into the kitchen, a wave of garlic hit her as she opened the door.

"My God, Steve. What is it?"

"If you really want to know, it is called Daube Cevenole. I made it last night actually. It improves with keeping and being heated up."

He kissed the tips of his bunched fingers and then ripped the cork from a bottle of red wine for the table.

After dinner Mary touched Steve's arm. "It can only have been Koll."

"Yes. Only Koll. Rather the people working for him. That only adds to our troubles. We are up against the Nazi old-boy network."

"It gives me the creeps," Mary said. "But it makes me boiling mad. Poor Dad. Poor darling Dad. He was one of the six million but he got away. And after all he went through, they still got him in the end. For every reason in the world, Koll has to suffer for that."

"But what can we do? There is simply nothing to go on. So far there is not even any evidence that your father is dead."

Mary looked defiant. "That's one thing that can be done. I've asked a private detective agency today to try to trace an X-ray photo which would show that piece of shrapnel. That would change the whole picture. Things like that don't get thrown away."

"War time," he shrugged. "Might have got destroyed by a V-2."

"All you do is pour cold water on the whole thing."

"Somebody has to look at it clearly and see what a tough proposition it is. You'll get no help from the British police and as for the West Berlin police, we've seen their style."

Mary tapped the pile of things at the end of the table that had come from her father's deed box in Goldfield's office: Viner's letters, deeds of the Flask Avenue house, a hundred or so pages of an unfinished and badly written manuscript about Viner's experiences in Sachsenhausen, the Viners' marriage certificate, Mary's birth certificate.

"Don't you think that if the British police saw this stuff they would do something?"

Steve shook his head slowly, lips pouted. "Don't be so naïve. They wouldn't lift a finger. None of it is evidence."

He paused and said: "Look, Mary. I'd like to tell you something, but only if you promise never to let it be known in any way."

"What is it?"

"Promise?"

"I have to. Yes. I promise."

"Gullet made me promise him. I could look for another job and never find it if he knew I'd told you."

"I've promised," Mary said.

"Okay. I happened to read the note attached to the report of the West Berlin police—by accident. Gullet caught me and he was furious. I said it was confidential and I would never let it go any further.

"Well. It said that your father had been making contacts in West Germany and West Berlin, contacts of a curious kind and as a result he had been kept under observation. It said that he had been in touch with the East Berlin authorities and was regarded by the West Berlin police as possibly an agent of the Communists. Gullet said he reckoned that things got a bit hot and your father slipped over to East Berlin and that accounts for his disappearance."

"You know that's utterly crazy. You've read his letters."

Steve said: "Whatever I or you may believe, you can see how the British police are going to react if you go to them now. And on top of that, a totally unsupported charge against one of the biggest West German industrialists, just when we are crawling to get into the Common Market. Hopeless!"

Mary downed a whole glass of wine in one and said: "But you yourself have said we should try to get Koll's fingerprints and prove that he is Kessel."

"Or that he isn't. Do you imagine that the British police would ask their pals in West Berlin to get them for us?"

"You pour cold water on everything."

"I'm only being realistic. Do you want to finish up like your father?"

Mary sat looking at her empty plate.

"Okay, Steve," she said bitterly. "I get your point."

"What point?"

"Don't be innocent, Steve. But I'm not going to drop this now."

"Did I say you should?"

"No, you—you hypocrite."

He got up again and paced, stopped and looked at her. She gave him back a hard stare.

"I said hypocrite, Steve. You didn't say it in as many words but that's the message. Well, I'd sooner die than give up now."

"One person already has."

"Has what?"

"Died."

She said furiously: "What's that, compared with living with what I would have to live with if I just got on with my highly intellectual job, writing mind-dulling trash for Mrs. Gullett and other coppers' wives and carving my career as a twaddle purveyor?"

"It's a job."

"Oh, my God! And I thought you were taking an interest."

Steve sighed patiently and said: "But you've got to face the facts. Can't you see the impossibility of it all? Even if you had much more than you've got. And you don't have to be so toffee-nosed about the *Phoenix* job. You were keen enough on it and you have to live."

"Don't you worry about me, Steve." Mary dabbed her eyes and looked at the resulting black. "I've already told Helen. She took it badly, but she took it. She can't guarantee my job will stay open but she'll do her best. I've told the solicitor I want to raise £2,000 on the house. It's worth £10,000 and I can repay it over the years. I can get another job. Not so good maybe, but I won't starve."

"But what would you do?"

"What *will* I do? Go back to Berlin. Start again. Maybe contact that fellow Dietrich."

"What do you know about him?"

"Now don't start again, Steve. If you've no ideas of your own, don't put the damper on mine."

Both sat silently—her silence pushing at him to go. If they had been anywhere else—at his flat or in a pub—she would have left. It was up to him. The pressure grew for him to do or say something. A phase was ending. Now he must either join the men or stay with the boys. He wanted neither. If he went now, it would be the end and he would regret it.

He went out of the room and put his coat on. In the process

he slipped into the garlic-smelling kitchen and poured a big gin down his throat from the bottle.

Back in the hallway, he could see her still sitting in the same position, lonely but not forlorn, her shoulders willing him to go. She did not look up. He balled his fists in frustration. Using what had been Harold Viner's key, he held back the spring of the lock so that the door would not make a noise and grimaced at his own cowardice as he closed it quietly.

On the Underground he thought about it all. Where was he going? Into loneliness, evenings in pubs, sexual satisfaction whenever it chanced along without strings. Suddenly his heart started to beat faster and he could scarcely wait to get out and take the next train back to Hampstead. He walked down the hill, still in time for the pubs.

Indecision settled round him again and he went in and drank a double gin and then another.

He walked past the house in Flask Avenue, passing a policeman who looked at him in that hard police way. There was no light downstairs but a gleam came from the upper back room. Still undecided, he walked back. The policeman was standing on the corner, waiting. Even the police were putting pressure on him, to go or stay. To go or stay. He laughed. The great, arrogant, irresponsible male.

The policeman began to saunter back. Steve crossed the road and let himself in while the policeman stood watching.

"It's all right, Mary," he called, so that the policeman could also hear. "It's only me."

He ran upstairs.

Her bedroom door was open and she was sitting on the bed with a piece of paper in her hand, looking at him as he came on to the little landing. Spread over her bed were her father's notes and the other papers from the deed-box.

"Darling Mary," he said, pulling her to her feet and kissing her smudged face. "How could I have gone and left you, even for an hour. I know I simply can't live without you. I love you, Mary. I love you. I must have been mad."

"Steve," she whispered, "Steve, Steve, Steve." Her black smeared eyes filled again with tears. "I don't know how I could have stood it if you hadn't come back."

"Darling," Steve said in her ear, "that's all over. If you can still stand me, I'll never, never, ever, but never, go away again."

"Oh," she sighed. "This is nice, Steve. Keep on kissing my neck."

They sat on the bed and he took the piece of paper she was still holding.

She became serious again.

"Steve, darling," she said, "I've been going through hell tonight. I couldn't tell you about this earlier and after we started quarrelling it was hopeless. But just look at that."

It was her birth certificate.

He looked puzzled, trying to find something significant on the lined form.

"Well, you were born. Weren't we all?"

"Look at the date."

"November 30, 1945. Blimey, what do you want for your birthday."

"It's far from a joke, Steve," she said in a preoccupied voice. "Sachsenhausen was not liberated till April. I'm quite sure of that."

Steve counted on his fingers.

"Seven months," she said. "I've worked it out."

"Plenty of premature babies get born."

"I weighed seven and a half pounds. My mother said what a bonny baby I was in spite of everything."

"But I don't see. . . ."

"You're getting warm, Steve."

"What do you mean?"

"Dad could not possibly have been my father."

"Don't be a fool."

"I am not. I never saw this certificate before. I realized as soon as I saw the date. God knows why it never occured to me before. I suppose there was no need to think about it. But Dad was either in solitary confinement or hidden under a pile of coal until the very day the Russians marched into the camp. Mother was in another part of the camp where she had been rescued from the SS and hidden. They met later in Berlin."

Steve stared at the crumpled paper.

"I don't see . . ." he began.

"It's clear enough. My actual father must have been an SS guard."

She wrapped her arms round him and wept great deep sobs as he stroked her hair.

"Can you understand, Steve," she said brokenly, "that I can't possibly live normally till I have done all I can to make life unbearable for Koll. I want to see that man behind bars. If that can't be done, I want to stigmatize him so that no decent person would go near him. I can't take revenge on the whole SS but here is one we know about.

"You should not think I don't know the risks involved. That's why, in a way, I was glad when you went. Why should I drag you into the mess? All the more so because I love you so much."

Stroking her bedraggled face, Steve said: "All that business of you and me has stopped as far as I am concerned—tonight. From now on it's we. And I want us to go on."

EIGHT

WEST BERLIN

At KaDeWe Steve took the lift to the sixth floor. The lift was full of the smell of the grocery department which entirely covers the top floor. In this lift it was bacon, in others onions.

On the sixth floor is a self-service restaurant.

It is a good place to arrange appointments. If the other party has not shown up it is possible to get a drink and also to do the shopping. It was also the one place in West Berlin which Steve felt absolutely confident of finding, based on his previous visit. Mary was late, but perhaps her plane was late.

With the skill of an experienced drinker, Steve had already discovered that the spirit to drink in Germany was Korn.

He was wedged in between a girl eating bockwurst and a man energetically hacking at a schnitzel at one of the stand up tables. Mary slid an arm through his and got a glare and a sharp elbow from the bockwurst eater.

Steve hastily swallowed his Korn and said: "Let's get out of here."

They went down in one of the bacon-smelling lifts and out through a side door. Steve stopped a taxi just as it was taking off.

"Maison de France," he said. He stopped Mary asking questions and said it was the only place apart from KaDeWe that he knew how to ask for.

They walked down Uhlandstrasse some way and turned

into a door between shops, up a flight of stairs and stopped at a flat bearing the nameplate Dr. Arvid Flintz. Steve opened the door with a key on a ring full of others. Inside, Steve shut the door and put his arms round Mary.

"That was a nice clinch," she said a minute later. "Now tell me what it's all about."

"This is where we live."

He led the way in like an estate agent. It was a typical flat of the Kaiser period, built for the well-to-do, but it had been converted with taste and without regard to expense. The effect was of warmth, peace and luxury.

"Steve, we're not made of money. What's it cost?"

"Nothing. Not a penny. Not even a pfennig. Jack Scutts, our man in Berlin, happened to have it lying about." He kissed her. "I'll give you a briefing.

"When I got here yesterday I saw Jack and told him what we agreed. I have an offer from a publisher to do a quickie thriller on Berlin—it would be under a different name and I hadn't told the *Success* why I wanted my holiday now. He won't say a word back at the office."

"And me?" Mary asked.

"You are Maria Schmidt. You are my interpreter and general help. I call you Mary because I don't like Maria. We met in London and you are working for me rather for love than gelt."

"Blackleg," Mary said. "I'll report this to the union."

"You are a West German, bi-lingual in English. But you haven't much money, nor I, so I asked Scutts if he could find you a room somewhere—cheap—where they wouldn't object to male visitors, papers or work permits.

"So Scutts said that this pal of his, Dr. Flintz who's an expert on something or other, would be away three months somewhere lecturing and had given his keys to Jack to clear the postbox and so on and we could have it if we wouldn't set fire to it."

Steve asked: "Do you know what this means?"

"Tell me."

"It means we don't have to register in a hotel and thus inform Herr Staengel that we are in town. Nobody will know we are here. That means, Koll doesn't know."

An hour later she came from the bathroom.

"God God," Steve said. "I'd never have known you."

"Nor will Staengel."

In place of her long cascade of almost black hair, short light brown waves nestled into the nape of her neck and fell round and over her forehead, touching the rims of round tortoise-shell glasses. She had changed her eye make-up and instead of her normal pallor, her skin had a warm reddish tint.

He walked around her.

"Wonderful, Mary. Shame about your hair. It'll grow out though."

She tweaked it and the wig came off and her own dark hair fell on her shoulders.

"Dyeing hair is old fashioned," she said.

Jack Scutts held his hand out as he came into the room and Mary took it and answered "Schmidt" to his "Scutts". Steve, pouring drinks in the corner, said: "What cher!"

Scutts looked too young to be on foreign assignment—not more than thirty—though with the normal journalistic signs of a misspent youth. He had loafed from job to job and found himself as clerk and junior representative in the Berlin office of a London firm, improving his school German and enjoying the atmosphere of the so-called front-line city. In the crisis of 1961, he had helped the chief foreign reporter of the *Success*, who spoke no word of any other language than English and

English itself not too well. Slowly Scutts broadened his experience and contacts, gave up his clerking job and was now the *Daily Success* correspondent in West Berlin.

He looked at the Scotch Steve poured for him and said: "Sorry. If I'm driving, I'll have to say no."

Steve stared at him, incredulous.

"It's a fact," Scutts said. "Just got my licence back. It was impounded for a year and I got six months sentence in clink, suspended. Someone rammed me from behind but I'd had a drink. If I cop it again I'll have to do the stretch and lord knows what else."

Steve pushed the glass into his hand. "It's taxis tonight, chum, and we're paying."

Scutts planned the evening. A few drinks and then an eisbein, followed by one or two night bars.

"What's an eisbein?" Steve asked.

"You will see. It is the one German dish that is truly German, unique, inimitable and between you and me, a marvellous dish in the winter months."

He led the way into Kurfürstendamm.

In a side street a large "antique" pub advertised its own freshly made sausages, home-cured hams and Bavarian specialities all from its own slaughterings and all, Scutts said, guaranteed delivered fresh each day from a factory somewhere.

Inside, bitter-faced waitresses were dressed in dirndles and starched frills and the men in green felt vests and leather aprons.

The eisbeins arrived.

"These aren't portions?" Steve whispered. "It's not possible."

Each eisbein was a huge wobbling pig's knuckle—bone, meat, fat and skin—gently simmered till it was ready to fall off the bone and occupying the place of honour on a thick china plate, divided into zones by raised rims like the banks of rice paddies. In the other three sections were piled sauerkraut, pease pudding topped with fried onion and plain boiled potatoes, floury and steaming.

After they had eaten. "It is a regrettable fact," Scutts said, "that unless you have been to the Chez Nous, you haven't really seen West Berlin. But I warn you—to get in and out and drink one Scotch won't cost much less than 100 marks for the three of us."

"It's only money," Mary said. "Steve will have to regard it as expenses—background for his book."

"It's not far. Let's walk the eisbein down," Scutts suggested.

Chez Nous was a plush and brocade, *fin-de-siècle* night bar with dim lighting and an aura of homosexuality as false as it was thick.

"It is," Scutts remarked, "a place where dull and stupid people come for a naughty evening."

They picked their way between tight-packed groups of moneyed provincials drinking sekt at 80 marks a bottle and as they sat down an elderly clown in drag with a vast bust and a voice like a rusty chain had his willing audience in convulsions with a piece of wit about blowing up his bosom with a foot pump.

When it finally came, the 15-mark-a-nip Scotch was smooth as surgical spirit.

"It doesn't actually kill," Scutts said.

Each succeeding item of the floor show seemed to have been dredged up from a lower level of slime than the one before. Their common qualities were amateurishness and abnormality.

They had paid their bill and were ready to go when Scutts

said: "Hang on! This chap coming in . . . . you should meet him."

He was fiftyish and running to fat and had just paid his entrance fee when he caught Scutt's wave. He strolled over— a man-about-town. Scutts introduced him: "Ralf Haase."

"Big honour for the Chez Nous," he said. "Where you been, Jack? Long time no see." He was proud of his nearly perfect English and especially of his Americanisms. When he crossed his legs it brought his silk socks and Bally shoes to notice. Everything was West German bourgeoise *comme il faut*—big gold cufflinks, tropical weight suit, white shirt. He ordered Bourbon for himself and three more whiskies.

"Unusual joint to find you in," Scutts remarked.

"Too right. Tourist trap. Brooks Brothers prices and Woolworth goods. Who are your new pals?"

"Steve, here, is the top crime reporter for my own paper. He's here to write a book about Berlin. I suppose the usual— brave clever British spies and stupid brutal Communists."

Haase groaned theatrically. "Not another one. I thought the market had fallen through. What is it this time? Smuggling a Russian space-craft through Checkpoint Charlie disguised as a circus elephant?"

"Steve reckons he's got a good plot."

"Actually," Steve said, thinking it was time to say something. "It's not even such a good idea, if it comes to that. But I've got a contract."

Haase laughed. "Lovely to be a writer, pay first and then. . . ." He shrugged.

Scutts said: "But seriously, Ralf. Nobody knows as much about Berlin as you do. You'll help this poor struggling author?"

Haase took a card from his pocket and dropped it on the table in front of Steve.

"Give me a ring," he said as he got up.

"Surely you were joking?" Mary said when he had gone. "How could a man like that help Steve?"

"No joke." Scutts was already fairly drunk.

"He is an old-hand Gehlen man. He specializes on the homo side. Been in a lot of big deals since the war."

"Be nice if I knew what a Gehlen man was," Steve put in.

Scutts laughed. "And you're going to write a book about Berlin. Still they say two weeks anywhere is enough to write a book. After that you start to realize you don't know much about the place."

"Tell him what a Gehlen man is," Mary said, as though she knew.

"Take too long and this joint is getting on my nerves. In a word it's the West German secret service, taken over lock stock and barrel from *Der Fuehrer*. For God's sake let's get out of here."

NINE

AGENT

S T E V E refused to hear of going to East Berlin.

"I am a silly English journalist who is going to write still another book about the super-spies of West Berlin and you are my helpmate, Maria Schmidt. Nobody knows we are here. By that I mean, Koll doesn't know we are here. I want to keep it that way."

"But surely we ought to let those people know that Koll and Kessel are the same man. It's unreasonable not to tell them. They are making enquiries too and may be wasting time and man-power on the wrong lines."

"No," said Steve. "Those fellows are politicians. As soon as they knew it they might go and broadcast it to the world."

"Is that such a bad thing?"

"That's something that could be done any time. But it won't get results. Hardly a month rolls by without the East Germans announcing that this or that big-shot in Bonn is former Nazi party card-holder No. 1234567 and what happens?"

"Nothing, I suppose," Mary answered dutifully.

"More than nothing. All the rest of the old-boy network rallies round and pats him on the back. That's the way it goes."

Steve finished his beer and ordered another. They were sitting well back from the pavement in Kranzlers and Mary was relishing a coffee that left nothing to be desired.

"Publicity won't get results," Steve went on. "The time may come when publicity is the only thing to fall back on. Let's hope not. What we have to do is find proof that Koll is Kessel and also the murderer of an Englishman who was a former prisoner in the camp where Kessel was a guard. Then the British authorities would have to sit up and take notice."

"Go on Sexton Blake," Mary said. "You're on form."

Encouraged by the sound of his own voice, Steve was getting enthusiastic.

"This could be important. First: prove that Koll is Kessel; second: prove that Koll murdered an Englishman who could have exposed him. Right. Koll is the leading figure in West Germany in the scheme to share production of Uranium 235 with Britain and Holland. My God! What a story! What a scandal! Mary, this is big stuff. It will make a hole bigger than an H-bomb."

Awed and carried away, Mary said: "You think it is really possible?"

"Darling. This could be the great story of the year. If we can bring this off we'll be making history."

"You're keen now," she said. "When it was only a matter of tracking down my father's murderer it was quite a different thing."

"Mary, darling, take what the Lord offers. I came with you because it was you. Whither thou goest, there go I and all that. But now I am in up to my ears. This is something bigger than I ever tackled. We could spike their guns, my sweet, with thick unremovable nails. We could put a spoke in their wheel."

"Just the same," Mary said dubiously, "I wonder whether the people in East Berlin could not help too."

"Maybe they could. But I'd prefer to keep the whole thing

in our hands. If we told them what we know about Koll being Kessel we simply could not be sure that it wouldn't leak. It would ruin the whole impact. This has to hit the world like a bomb. Can't you see that? Headlines in every paper. Day after day."

"Yes and no. It all depends on whether we have the means to bring it off. I'm not so sure. As far as you're concerned, it's a newspaper story now."

"It's the kind of story that can topple governments."

"Okay, Steve," Mary agreed. "I'd sooner have you in this mood than the other. Let's take it from here. Where do we start?"

He flicked at his white cuff. It was half past four.

"We don't have much time for anything today. I'm taking Scutts' pal to supper. No. Don't say it. I don't really expect much from him but I'd like to pump him on a couple of points, and it helps my alibi if I seem to be getting material for a book."

"Okay, Steve. Don't protest so much. And what should the little woman do?"

"How about Scutts' files. We should have everything that's available about Koll. But don't let him see that it's really Koll we're interested in. Go through other files as well. We'll get down to some planning tomorrow."

Mary set off through the sunlight of Kurfürstendamm, a fugitive from Koll, living incognito, but hunting him too. She saw herself in a shop and the short-haired stranger with glasses who stared back gave her more confidence.

Haase knew about food. He had suggested Schlichters, a small old-fashioned eatery away from the centre. It had been a splendid meal—caviar, a perfect Chateaubriand, Chateauneuf, Danish Blue, coffee, cognac, cigars. Ralf Haase ate and drank gluttonously, belched occasionally and as his alcoholic level rose, his darting eyes slowed to become more fixed. His mealtime talk had been of his wartime adventures. As their second cognac came, Steve intervened.

"Scutts told me that nobody knows so much as you about Berlin."

"Na," Haase said modestly. "That goes too far. All the same, I've been on the inside track of a lot of Berlin history. The good old days. Things have not been so good since the Wall. Waiter!"

He ordered two more cognacs.

"Okay," said Haase. "What do you want to know? You aren't British Intelligence, I suppose?" It was a joke and he laughed heartily about it as though the idea of Steve being Intelligence was excruciating.

Steve joined the laugh. He tossed his National Union of Journalists card on the table.

"Tchah!" Haase tossed it back. "Lend me that for twenty-four hours and I'll have a dozen like it made."

"Now that's interesting," Steve said. "That kind of thing is what I need for my book."

"Ah, yes, of course, your book. Books about Berlin. If it's an American author, the brains are all in the C.I.A. If it's a British writer, then M.I.6 unlocks all the secrets. Nobody ever seems to write about the B.N.D.[1] or the M.A.D.[2] not to mention the B.V.S.[3] They are the ones that really run the show."

He grinned, shrugged his shoulders and went on: "What harm does it do to let everyone think that the Germans are

[1] B.N.D. Bundesnachrichtendienst—Federal Intelligence Service. Successor to the Gehlen Bureau.
[2] M.A.D. Militaerischer Abschirmdienst—Military Counter-Intelligence.
[3] B.V.S. Bundesverfassungsschutz—Civilian Intelligence.

fools? But your book—what do you want to know? Little Tommy Tucker must sing for his supper."

Another cognac went down and Steve pushed over one of his.

"Just a couple of things. For example, is it possible to buy a British passport in West Berlin?"

Haase stared at him. Here was a right one.

"In West Berlin you can buy any kind of passport you want. This is the main world centre of the business." He spoke with a certain pride. "We had a lot of practice after the war. There were people who for one or other reason simply had to leave Germany. Quite a lot needed to change their identity. Of course the big rush died away and only the experts stayed in the private trade."

"Private trade?" Steve looked puzzled.

"Intelligence services naturally make their own," Haase said.

Steve ordered two more cognacs. "What would a British passport cost and how would you go about getting one?"

"What kind? False-real or real-false?"

"You're the expert. You tell me."

"Well, British passports are very expensive. Very much so." His diction was deliberate. The cognac was getting to him. "A British passport takes you almost anywhere and it lasts ten years, so nobody takes any notice if they look dirty and worn. All to the good. But they are hard to alter or forge.

"Now take a false-real British passport—a genuine British passport, that is, but with the original entries removed by chemical means and new entries made, new photo, new embossing, which is quite an art in itself. I reckon it would cost you today," he wrinkled his nose and counted on his fingers, "rock bottom, 2,500 marks. More likely 4,000 to

5,000 marks depending on the state of the market. Sometimes they simply are not to be had."

"And the other kinds?"

"Real-false—forged from start to finish so that a lot depends on the quality of the workmanship. Some, like German whisky, would not deceive a teenager. You can't use them to get into or out of Britain but they pass muster generally. Prices vary between 800 and 1,500 marks. Unless you can get one made by one of the intelligence services. They have been known to come on the market. But as they are almost as good as originals they cost about the same."

He pondered, drank most of another cognac and washed it down with soda water.

"If your book needs a passport for a secret agent, well of course, the services make their own."

Steve shook his head. "No spies. That phoney spy racket is old hat now."

"What's the other thing?"

"Suppose my chief character wanted to trace two or three men who had crossed over into East Berlin in a car and come back on the same day—been up to some monkey business with the East Germans. Would he be able to trace them?"

Haase took a long time thinking this over.

"Not agents?"

"No. Let's say industrial. Trying to stop someone doing business with the East Germans, maybe."

"Would they be Germans or foreigners?"

"West Germans, I imagine."

"What car? Not a Volkswagen, I hope."

"Would have to be a biggish car. Maybe stolen. False plates. Have to reckon with all that."

"The day is known?"

"Yes."

"Would the men concerned have false West German papers, too?"

"I should think so."

Haase leaned forward and rested his flabby chin on manicured hands.

"The people here pretend that they don't pay any attention to comings and goings across the Berlin border. They say that they don't recognize it as a border so how can they bother with it. Actually they do though and they even arrest West Berliners for buying Scotch and cigarettes in East Berlin. There would be a fair chance of tracing them through official channels."

"Privately?"

"You'd need to find the right person to bribe."

"Could you find that person?"

"Possibly, if I needed to." He looked at his watch.

"One more point. How easy is it to smuggle a man into and out of East Berlin from here?"

"Easy? How easy? How hard, rather." Haase laughed. "You mean really smuggle—in a car or a coffin, like the paperbacks?"

Steve nodded.

Haase burst into loud peals of laughter. When he finally got his mirth under control, he shook his head, wiped his eyes and said: "No. No. My friend. No."

"It's not on?"

"Not on? Ah, of course, a new piece of slang. Not possible, you mean. A neat expression I must say. You're right, it's not on. Ninety nine point nine recurring per cent sure that you would get caught, whatever the paperbacks say. Those East Berlin *Grepos*[1] know all those tricks."

"What about in an Allied military vehicle?"

[1] Grepo: Grenzpolizei. Border police.

"Theoretically possible. In practice you may rule it out. Army drivers don't just pop over there when they feel they'd like some fresh air. Control this side is tight. Such an operation would have to be either official or you'd have to corrupt the whole personnel in the car. And how could you ever know whether a chance would come to dump your man on the other side? Or get him out?"

Steve said: "He would get out another way."

"Then what are we talking about? Getting in is no problem. A West German passport, dirt cheap, would get you in. The fly in the ointment is that once you've been in East Berlin for twenty-four hours, unless you have an East German foreign Ministry visa, your papers are automatically out of order."

He finished the last of his cognac and looked at his watch again but was carried on by his theme.

"The Berlin border remains the best way to penetrate the G.D.R. and also, given well-forged papers, to penetrate the other countries on its borders—Czechoslovakia, Poland, others too. Then the problem arises—how to get back?"

Haase looked at his watch again, belched, looked at his empty glass and said: "You're a writer. You can solve all problems with your pen. The people on the ground have real problems to contend with."

"They risk their lives," Steve said.

"It's one way to earn a living."

Haase led the way to Wittenberg Platz through side streets reminiscing about the good old days before the Wall.

On the way he stopped suddenly and said: "Off the record. Not for the book. You see that antique shop over there?"

It was an old-fashioned double-fronted shop, jammed with

assorted junk, under the sign Antiquitaeten—Peter Metz-schuk.

Haase walked on.

"That is one of the front men for the biggest passport dealers in West Berlin. Be warned: It's a dangerous little bunch. I don't advise you to drop in and ask innocent questions about getting false papers. You have to be introduced."

TEN

KOLL'S FINGERPRINTS

MARY VINER'S notes on Josef Koll:

1945 : Hamburg. Ex-corporal (Wehrmacht) Josef Koll offered his services to the British forces.

Spoke English. Obviously a gentleman. Pleasant, quiet, reserved, sparing drinker.

Was asked why only a Wehrmacht corporal. Seemed he was not a Nazi supporter. Type of good German conservative. Anti-Communist and anti-Nazi. Became ordinary soldier to avoid being involved with the Nazis.

His view : Hitler had not understood that Britain, France, Germany and other western powers needed to have joined forces against the Russians.

This was exactly the kind of German the allies were looking for—no Nazi past, conservative.

Koll helped the British forces and they helped him. He got licences to start enterprises and found the capital for them.

By 1952 Koll was one of the richest of the new post-war rich. Interests range over very wide field : flour, groceries, building, liquor, banking, shipping.

Long involved in pilot development of nuclear power projects and these, with his close relations with Bonn Ministers put him in the centre of the plans for developing the gas-centrifuge method of enriching uranium.

Personally, Koll is hardworking and abstemious. Unmarried.

Member of C.D.U. Heavy subscriber to C.D.U. funds. Makes no political pronouncements.
It is said (not by him) that he moved his business headquarters to Berlin as a demonstration—to emphasize that Germany would again be reunited with Berlin as its capital.
Born Amberg, May 5, 1915. Named Franz-Josef. Parents died in a fire in Amberg in 1945.

Mary came popping along toward the flat, light, tall, slender and graceful on slim, booted legs. As Steve watched her from the window, she dodged illegally across the road against a traffic light. He must warn her against this. As he watched a policeman advanced purposefully from behind her. If he stopped her, the first question would be for her papers. Her name would flash through the computer at how many millions of miles per second and land on Staengel's desk. The policeman was only three yards behind her when she turned into the flat entrance below. He slowed down, evidently deciding it was not worth the candle.

Filled with relief, Steve had the door open and was kissing her before she was inside.

"Steve, darling, you'll never guess." She pulled away, full of excitement. "You'll never guess. I've found out where the porter lives. You know," she said when he looked puzzled, "the one at the Ebert who handed over my father's bag. I passed the Ebert on my way from Scutts' place and suddenly I had the idea to try the reception clerk with a ten mark note. Worked like a charm, as usual. Reinhardt Singer, Sylter Strasse 7, Wedding."

"Let's go and see him, right now."

"Might be at work."

"Might not. He's a night porter, if that is a profession."

The telephone settled it.

"Hallo, Jack," Steve said.

"Hallo to you," Scutts answered. "What's your interest in Koll?"

"Koll? Why, Koll?" Steve looked at Mary.

"Because your gorgeous assistant spent so long on the file."

"Are you sure she hadn't fallen asleep? Anyway, he's an interesting figure isn't he?"

"I suppose you haven't discovered that he is really Martin Borman and are keeping the news for your book."

"How did you guess? Actually, I thought you said he was one of the few big shots around here who had no Nazi past."

"Do you want to meet him?"

Steve paused, almost too long. "It would be a good idea. Privately, you mean?"

"Come off it. I'm not *The Times* or the Foreign Office and even they are too small beer for Herr Koll. No. He is guest of the Foreign Journalists' Association for lunch today. Slumming. Still he has to keep in with the press. Background talk. Off the record. Like to come?"

"Can you fiddle me in?"

"Visiting fireman. Cost you fifteen marks for the lunch. I suppose you know he is the chief pusher in the gas centrifuge caper?"

"I hadn't realized it," lied Steve.

"Schoeneberg Rathaus, then, at 1.15 for 1.30."

As he put the phone down Steve said softly: "My God! The ice seems to be cracking."

Current chairman of the Foreign Journalists Association was a nasal-voiced B.B.C. man who honked a welcome at Steve and passed him to a female secretary who was busy in several directions at once but did not forget to tap him for the fifteen marks for lunch. It was well-attended. At these lunches influential and sometimes well-informed people could anonymously push their own line by talking informally to journalists whom they knew would not quote them.

At 1.30 exactly the door flung open and Josef Koll walked in.

His first sight of Josef Koll hit Steve with shock and almost disappointment. Many people claim that they can read character from people's faces and it may sometimes be true. Nature provides a man with the bone and general shape of his features, but his face, his habitual expression in later life owes much to his hopes and fears, the breadth or narrowness of his ideals, his social or anti-social attitudes.

Steve, studying Koll, found himself at a loss.

Slim, erect, walking round to the top table with calm grace and confidence, enhanced by a quiet, superbly cut dark suit, expensively tanned, easy and without arrogance. From the first glance Koll was a man of distinction, chatting lightly with the chairman, laughing, friendly and in command. Steve tried and failed to visualize him as SS Hauptsturmfuehrer Wolfgang Kessel, sadistic guard at Sachsenhausen.

Steve felt real personal hatred for the man growing in him. It was unjust that he should not carry his evil in his face, that he should be so handsome, so charming and so rich.

The waiters began serving venison with red cabbage and apple and creamed potatoes.

The chairman stood up.

"Meine Damen und Herren: Today we have two guests. . . ."

Steve kicked himself for not having thought of this and warned Scutts.

". . . We all know our guest of honour and I need only thank Herr Koll for coming here today. Our other guest is a colleague of Jack Scutts—Mr. Blake."

Scutts nudged him to stand up.

He bobbed up and down, watching Koll, but there was no change of expression. Now he saw that this was in fact the characteristic of his face, as though the features were obeying instructions to remain in a pose. He observed also that when he caught it in repose, the face became full-lipped, petulant and weak.

German was the common language of the journalists and without knowing the language, Steve felt that he spoke it well. Scutts interpreted. Koll got a lot of laughs at the expense of the Soviet Union and to a less extent the U.S.A. Such powers, he said, were trying to prevent the "have not" or "have less" powers from the peaceful exploitation of nuclear power and all its many-sided by-products. The Federal Republic would never make use of nuclear weapons except as a means of defence. Nor would it tolerate being a second-class power. It was time to draw a line under the recriminations of the past. The Germans had overcome their past and were marching in the vanguard of the democratic nations.

He spoke without notes. When pausing for a thought, he had the habit of sliding his fingers over his chin. Then he would rest his hands on the table as he leaned forward to speak. They rested often on his place card.

Koll's place card became the centre of Steve's world.

Coffee came and cognac and cigars. It was breaking up. Koll in any case had an appointment. Full of respectful bonhomie the balding B.B.C. man escorted the guest of honour to the door. Steve stood up with others and moved round to the top table. He wiped his hands on his handkerchief and dropped it over Koll's place card. He picked them up together with a sigh of relief.

"Don't count your chickens, Mary. Suppose his dabs show that he isn't Kessel at all."

Mary kissed him again. "It was still very smart of you. But I think they will prove that father was right. He should have known if anyone should."

Steve spread out a newspaper on the kitchen table and carefully got Koll's place card out. He had turned it inside out on the fold. Lampblack and fixative he had bought at an artists' shop and a little rubber puffer such as they use for giving enemas to babies at a Drogerie.

He cut the card in two, holding it only at the corner with tweezers and put half in the centre of the newspaper. He puffed lampblack in the air from some distance letting it fall lightly and gradually build up to an even black. Then he blew the lampblack away.

Fingerprints stood out clear and bold, some obliterating others, some alone and sharp.

Steve developed the other card with similar results and fixed them carefully with an aerosol from a distance to avoid smudging.

As soon as they were dry he put the copy of the Dresden police prints by the side of the Koll place card and compared the first of the new prints with a lens.

"Look at this, Steve." Mary pointed to the Dresden copy of Kessel's forefinger, excitedly. "It's just like this one."

The print on Koll's place card was almost complete and rather sharp. It was distinguished by an irregular wavy line, very faint, on one side. This was a scar, very cleanly healed but it had at one time cut clean across the arches. It was also present on the Dresden print. Kessel's forefinger and Koll's forefingers were the same.

Steve whispered: "My God, we've done it! We've done it! We hardly have to look at the rest."

Mary danced round the kitchen table, went out, came back with her coat.

"I'm going out to get a bottle of champagne," she stated. "And then I propose we go to bed."

Steve looked at his watch.

"Don't look at your watch, you," she said. "Oh, of course. I remember. We have to see the porter.

ELEVEN

DEATH IN WEDDING

REINIE SINGER'S home was on the top floor of an ancient house in Wedding. A row of rusty tin postboxes in the dank hallway bore the faded names of tenants and subtenants.

A scrap of paper stuck behind a bell push carried the name Singer, but the button produced no result and knocking brought no answer.

"Let's ask over the way," Mary suggested.

There the bell produced a shuffling and the chink of a door chain. This allowed the door to open two inches through which peered anxious watery eyes topped by flimsy white hair, yellowish and dirty.

"*Na?*" she squeaked, without the usual *"Guten Abend."*

Mary apologized. "We're looking for Herr Singer."

"Over there." The door began to close.

"He's out."

"At work or in the pub."

"Which pub?"

The door had been steadily closing and as the old woman said: "Bierquelle," it shut and the feet shuffled away.

The Bierquelle was one of the squalid pubs now rare in Berlin and generally found only in the old slum quarters. It served the cheapest beer, spirits, bockwurst and pork rissoles.

Mary walked to the bar. The hostess was an enormous woman who in spite of her general fat had a sharp face like a hatchet and pale blue eyes, and simply jerked a thumb in the direction of a corner where a notice said: Toiletten.

Mary shook her head. "I'm looking for a Herr Singer. Herr Reinhardt Singer. Is he here?"

"Reinie," the woman called and a small man detached himself from the bar, wiping his mouth with the back of his hand.

Reinie was a devotee of weinbrand and beer. Seeing that it was free, he ordered a double Albach Uralt, the dearest they kept in the Bierquelle.

Reinie's appearance tended to explain why he had not risen above the rank of night porter in a pension. His overcoat had certainly belonged to someone else and under it a cotton roll-neck sweater in washed-out purple gave no other evidence of having been in water. He spoke German with a thick Berliner accent which Mary found hard to understand.

Steve asked: Did he want to make a bit of money? Mary translated.

He looked round the bar. What was it all about?

It was nothing to talk about here, Steve said.

Reinie looked worried. He knew of another pub.

No. No pubs. No cafés either. What about his own flat?

It was in a horrible mess. Anyway, what was it all about?

Steve said never mind the mess. His flat would do. They would go now. He paid and Reinie followed them out. He was not quite steady on his legs but gave no other sign of drink.

He was still dubious about going to his flat. Mary talked him round mainly by offering to get a bottle of weinbrand and some beer in the corner shop.

As he opened his flat door, Steve said: "Phew! What a stink."

It was cold inside. Two doors opened out of a tiny passage

but Reinie led the way into the ancient kitchen. He lit an old black gas oven and left the door open for warmth, pushing dirty plates and remnants of food back to the wall to clear some space on the lino-covered kitchen table.

Reinie at least made no apology for the state of affairs but opened the brandy and flicked the tops off three beer bottles which he handed round to be drunk in the German workers' manner.

"*Na?*" he said.

Mary told him her name but it did not register.

"*Weiner?*" he queried.

Mary told him who she was.

"*Scheisse!*" He put his bottle down. "You can both get out. I'm not getting mixed up with the bulls." He stood up and repeated: "Get out!"

Steve said: "Tell him to shut up and sit down. It's up to him whether he comes out with money in his pocket or in gaol."

"It's nothing to do with me. I've told the cops all I know."

Steve pulled out a club membership card with his photo on it and flashed it in front of Reinie.

"Scotland Yard," he said. "Mr. Singer, you don't seem to realize that this is a serious business. There were important documents in the Englishman's case and they have to be traced. I am co-operating with the German police. We have to find the man who got it from you."

Reinie poured himself another weinbrand and said sullenly: "I told the cops all I knew."

"Maybe you can tell us more. We want to know, anyway, what he looked like, how he spoke, how he was dressed and how he walked. We have to know everything about him because, come what may, we have to find him. Information is worth money to us."

Reinie said nothing.

"It's better for you to co-operate. I came first because I don't want to have to get it out of you at the police station. But if it comes to that. . . ." Steve shrugged.

"What do you mean by money?" Reinie asked.

"It depends on the information."

"How do I know I won't get dragged in anyway?"

"I want to keep it as quiet as possible too."

"And the money?"

"I'd pay 50 marks for a good description of the man."

Reinie nibbled his nails.

"Got a cigarette?" he asked.

Mary gave him one and lit it. The gas hissed. It was warm now and they had got used to the smell.

He poured another weinbrand and drank it, his hand shaking.

"What would his name be worth?"

Mary felt a thrill of excitement.

"Worth another 100. But watch it, Mr. Singer. Anyone can invent a name. Or a description. I'm after the truth. The only way to stay safe is to tell it." Steve swallowed a brandy for the look of it. It was a rough brew.

"What would the name and address be worth?"

"You told the police you did not know the man."

"Suppose I did now?" Reinie took another drink. It seemed to give him confidence. "What would that be worth?"

Mary said in English to Steve: "I think he's playing with us."

"That's what we have to find out," Steve answered. "Ask him whether he knows the name and address."

Reinie refused to answer this: "How much?" he said.

"Four hundred marks."

"Make it five."

Steve looked at Mary. It was her money. She nodded.

"Steve," she said, choosing words that were not like German, "if we can get this out, it must lead further. It's worth the cash, if he isn't cheating. That's the real trouble."

Steve did not say anything for a few moments. Then he took out a packet of fifty mark notes and peeled two off.

"That's to show we mean business." He waited for her to translate.

"Now I want to know how he found out the name and address of the man who called for the suitcase."

Reinie appeared to be trying to decide whether he was playing the right cards. Just to be sure, he took another drink. He was nervous and out of his depth but he had seen the money.

"After the cops came round I got the sack from the Ebert. Naturally."

"Why didn't you tell the police you knew the man?"

Reinie's mouth turned up a little in a grin.

"Because I didn't know then."

"Let him talk, Steve," Mary said.

"Anyway, they weren't interested. If they had been, they'd have taken me in and worked me over. Our cops don't pay for information."

Reinie asked for another cigarette and went on: "I didn't know this fellow. When I got the sack, I went to work at Ashinger's—corner of the Zoo station—clearing up dirty plates. Then this fellow came in. I nipped out to the back in case he spotted me. Had to have a think, too, see? If the cops was after him. . . . Well, he got himself a sausage and chips and stood there eating.

"I thought, there he is, wanted by the police. Why not make him pay a bit to keep it under wraps. I'd just been paid my wages. So I took my smock off and went AWOL. What's a job in Ashinger's anyway? I stood outside, watching him through the window. He finished his sausage and went out. I followed him round for a couple of hours, then he went to a cinema and I waited. Then I followed him home. Lives out in Neukolln."

Steve asked: "Did you try to touch him for money?"

"Nah. It was only a week ago. Less. I didn't want to do it on my own in case he had mates. I tried to get a pal to come in with me but he didn't like the idea because the cops were after this bloke."

"How do you know he hasn't moved?"

"I don't," Reinie admitted. "But I'll sell you the name and address for 500."

Mary said: "Do you think he made it up?"

"I don't think so. It's such a simple tale that I think it's genuine."

"I wouldn't trust him an inch."

"Me too." Steve pushed out his lower lip and squeezed his chin between thumb and fingers.

"The Thinker," Mary commented.

"Shut up. One of us has to think. OK. He's got a hundred marks. Here are 400 more." Steve took them from his pocket.

"Steve. Are you mad?" Mary put her hand out to stop him giving them to Reinie.

He deliberately tore them through the middle.

Reinie looked on in horror.

Steve put the eight halves of the fifty-mark notes on the table by Reinic's hand. The others he put back in his pocket.

"Now I want the address," he said.

Reinie went on looking at the halves, shaking his head. He had had enough but he poured another, spilling it on his fingers.

Steve picked up the torn pieces and pressed them into his hand.

"The other halves," he patted his pocket, "you get tomorrow. After we've checked the address."

"OK," Reinie said. "You'll bring them tomorrow?"

"I swear it."

"Seven o'clock. Here."

"No. Seven o'clock at Zoo Station post office."

"The man's name is Grell. Neukolln, Teupitz Strasse, 125, Second Floor."

It was half past eight. Steve and Mary stood outside Reinie's house in the dark talking like lovers for about fifteen minutes but there was no sign of Reinie.

"With the rest of that bottle of spirits and three bottles of beer, why should he go out?" Mary remarked.

"Maybe to warn Grell. Come on. Neukolln next stop."

Teupitz Strasse was a long walk from the station, running straight down to the Berlin border opposite Treptow Park. It was another dismal part of old Berlin with the standard fifty- or sixty-year-old type of flat dwellings, losing their plaster.

Germans are great lockers up. It is a custom stamped with the irrational inevitability of Prussian tradition, to lock all front doors at eight o'clock in the evening—to the great inconvenience of all concerned, except burglars. Special locks have been devised to foil the enemy of tradition whose aim it might be not to lock doors. In such cases, the key has to be pushed through the door and, with a bit at each end, can only be withdrawn when the door has been relocked.

Of course, the front door of 125 was locked.

Suddenly lights went on behind the door. Someone had pressed the minute switch. A shadow came on the frosted glass and a key turned.

As the door opened, Mary said: *"Guten abend"* and made to enter. The man coming out was tall and thin, wearing a hat and a muffler round his throat. It was not possible to see his face because the light came from behind.

"*Guten abend,*" he replied hoarsely. He pushed past, not standing aside to let Mary enter first and went down the stone steps. He was carrying a light suitcase.

"Herr Grell?" Mary asked.

The man stopped, pointed a finger upward and said: "Second floor."

He turned toward the station.

Mary and Steve looked at each other.

"I wonder . . ." Steve began.

Suddenly the lights went out and Steve had to fumble for the push button.

On the second floor, the left-hand flat had the name Grell written on the paint with a ball-point. They could hear the bell trilling inside as Steve kept his finger on it.

Nobody answered.

"I'll bet that was Grell we saw, blowing the coop," Steve said. "That little rat Singer must have gypped us."

The minute light went out.

Steve felt the door, which had a fixed handle outside. It had plenty of play.

"That handle's good," he whispered. "I'm for going in."

"I'm scared."

"We're the injured parties," Steve answered.

Steve had a tiny torch which he used as a car-key ring. In the tiny beam, Mary saw him insert a plastic or celluloid calender—an advertisement for the Chez Nous—between the door and the jamb.

He eased the door to him, pressing with the plastic sheet. There was a faint click. Mary slid in behind him. It was pitch dark.

Steve sniffed.

"Cigar." He sniffed again. "Pretty fresh too."

It was a typical flat of its kind. Four doors opening out of an irregularly shaped hallway. He opened one door. The curtains were drawn. In the tiny beam of the torch they could see that it was a bedroom, bed unmade, wardrobe open, drawers pulled out and left hanging open. It had a stale, old-man smell behind the cigar smell.

A saucer doing duty as an ashtray held some cigar ends and ash. Steve picked them up one by one, selected one, smelt it.

"This one is still warm. We let him walk out past our noses."

"Singer?"

"It must have been. Wanted the money. Then got cold feet. Took a taxi."

Only one other room was used and showed the same signs of hasty departure. A wet drip-dry shirt hung in the bathroom.

"Let's go and have a word with Brother Reinie," he whispered.

"I'll give that little swine something to be scared about."

"What's the use?" Mary said.

"He's still our only link with Grell. Maybe he'll still try to earn the rest of that 500, after proving that he is on Grell's side by tipping him off. Cunning little rat."

It was after eleven when they got back to the little cul de sac where Singer lived.

Steve put a hand on Mary's arm and they stopped. A police car was pulled across the street entrance and several more police formed a cordon on either side.

"Not our lucky night," Steve groaned. "Now what?"

"After coming all this way we'd better wait. They may go away."

They found a pub near the U-Bahn and sat near the bar.

A man came in and said: "*Gott sei dank* you're still open, Erne. Came off shift and couldn't get near the Quelle for cops. What's on?"

The woman behind the bar did not need any prompting.

"What? You haven't heard? There's been a murder."

"What down in Sylter?"

"That's right. What's yours? Sylter Strasse."

"*Donnerwetter!* That's my street. Pils and korn. Make it a double. Who was it?"

"I suppose you know him then. Little fellow name of Singer. Reinie Singer. Used to come in here sometimes. No better than he should have been, I'd say. Know him?"

"Reinie Singer. God! He lives next door. What happened?"

Catching the name but understanding nothing, Steve raised an eyebrow. Mary shook her head, not to miss anything.

The woman put down the man's beer and schnapps. She shrugged her shoulders.

"Well, what I heard," she leaned forward cheerfully confidential, "the people downstairs heard some noise and a bump, and a sort of yell. The man went and looked out of the spyhole in the door. He heard some people going down but they didn't put the stairwell light on so he didn't see them. He was scared and went to find the *hausmeister*. When they got in, there was Reinie Singer with a bit of paper stuffed in his mouth. Dead. Stabbed. Gang business, they say."

Mary moved her head in the direction of the door. Steve paid and they left.

Mary told Steve. "Poor little Reinie," she commented. "But it's curious, isn't it?"

"What do you mean? Curious?"

"All so quick."

At the next corner, Steve's hand stopped her.

E

"Ssh," he whispered.

He pressed himself flat against the house wall and edged his head sideways round it.

There was nobody but a weaving drunk.

"Steve, are we being followed?" she whispered.

"I don't think so. But you know what this means?"

"You mean poor Reinie getting. . . ?"

He nodded. "It means they are on to us."

TWELVE

DIETRICH SURFACES

I T wasn't till they reached the flat at one o'clock that they realized they were hungry.

"I'll have a perfect meal ready for you in ten minutes," Mary said.

Steve got his pistol from the toilet cistern, where it had been hung on a string, in a waterproof plastic bag since he got to Berlin, and went to join Mary in the kitchen.

He emptied the chambers of the pistol on to the table. "There's nothing in it now so it won't fire. This little thing here," he indicated the safety catch with his thumb, "stops it firing when you don't want it to. When it's back it won't fire. Like now."

He handed it to her. She pulled the trigger and the hammer rose and fell.

"But it is firing. If the bullets were in. . . ."

"No," he said. "The hammer is blocked and the pin can't hit the cartridge. Look."

He tore a thin strip off a visiting card and pushed it between the breech block and the magazine and pulled the trigger.

"See, no mark on the card. And now. . . ."

He pushed the safety catch forward and pulled the trigger again. When he pulled it out there was a hole in the card.

"If there'd been a cartridge in there, the hammer would have hit it and fired it and the bullet would have come out here. When the catch is back it won't fire. When it's forward, it fires. That's all."

"Horrible things."

He slipped the cartridges back into the cylinder and tried the steak tartare. "Marvellous. Chopped I see and not ground —and so good for my figure."

"Your what?"

Just then the doorbell rang.

Steve looked at his watch. It was after two a.m. He picked up the gun and put it in his pocket as he went to open the door.

A fattish man stood there with a letter in his hand. A taxi-driver.

"Fraulein Weiner?" he asked.

She nodded.

"I have to give you this."

She took the letter.

The man stood expectantly. Steve fished in his pocket and found a two-mark piece. Not happily, the man went.

The letter was very strongly sealed with tape and took a little time to open. It was typed and so was the signature— Franz Dietrich. She read it through once and then slowly translated it.

Dear Miss Viner,

I tried to telephone you in London some time ago and it has not been easy to trace you. I do not need to put too much in writing. I assure you that we both have the same purpose. It begins with K. We would gain by working together. I prefer not to call on you or telephone and I should like to meet Mr. Blake. I suggest the following meeting place. Please buy a Richard Schwarz map of greater Berlin (No. 30 costing 2 marks 50). Draw a straight

line between Police Post 150 (square G6) and Krumme
Lanke U-Bahn Station. Draw another between Grunewald
Turm and Johanna Platz. You will find that they intersect
at a crossing of two roads in Grunewald, in a straight line
from Teufelsee. If Mr. Blake will be at that point at
16.00 hours this afternoon, I will introduce myself. I know
him by sight.

Important: Mr. Blake must spend as long as may be
needed to ensure that he is not being followed. He must
be quite sure of that. If he seems to be tailed when he
reaches the rendezvous, I shall not appear.

Please take this very seriously. After what happened to R.S.
we shall have to work fast if we are to avoid a similar
mistake in regard to G.

Franz Dietrich.

"You're not going?" Mary asked.

"Certainly."

"It may be a trap!"

"I agree. Anyway, he seems to know what he's talking
about: R.S. and G. Reinie Singer and Grell."

"Maybe someone wants to have you out of the way to deal
with me alone."

Steve shook his head. "Go window shopping. Have a long
lunch in a very safe place—Kempinski's. Go to a cinema."

Steve's first call was at a small shop where he bought a
cheap raincoat and a cloth cap. There was nobody else in the
shop. He went out with the parcel under his arm and carefully avoided looking round to see if he was tailed. The only
shop he knew was KaDeWe so he hopped a taxi and asked
for it, stepping out immediately it drew up, money ready,
and into the shop. He caught a lift just going up and rode

it to the top, nipped out and caught one just going down. It stopped at the first and he got out, walked rapidly round the first floor, down the stairs and out of a side door, mixing with a crowd which was crossing to the U-Bahn station. A platform announcer was calling: "Ruhleben. Stand back!" He dived between the closing doors. Very few people got off at the terminus, leaving the train empty. He examined them carefully and waited till almost departure time before getting back into the train, peering out till the automatic doors slid past his nose. Getting out at Sophie Charlotte Platz he went straight into the nearest pub for a snack and from there could see a cinema advertising a film about the call-girl racket in Frankfurt on Main. Three marks got him a back seat in the almost empty cinema and after ten minutes he got up, crossed the back aisle and slipped out to the toilet. Nobody got up at the same time. In the toilet he put on his new pocket raincoat over his coat, rolled up his hat and put it in his pocket and walked out wearing his new cloth cap. By now he felt rather sure that he was clean but he still had plenty of time for a few aimless bus rides and walks along deserted streets before jumping into a passing taxi. No car followed and he paid the man off at Teufelsee.

The light was starting to fade when he reached the rendez-vous and there was nobody in sight. It was five to four. He walked at a stroller's pace past the intersection and then back.

A tall, athletically moving man was walking along the narrow road toward him.

"Mr. Blake," he said. "Good evening. My name is Dietrich."

They shook hands.

"I think we should continue walking," Dietrich said. His English was fair. Steve fell in alongside. Dietrich might have been Steve's age or older. He was well-dressed and self-confident in bearing. Good looking, tanned.

"Let us not waste time, Mr. Blake," he said. "I told Fraulein Viner in London that West Berlin is a place where it is very easy to make mistakes. One must know what one does. I fear that she disregarded this advice. And so, Grell was warned and Singer—well, you know what happened. It would have been possible to avoid if you had first made contact with me."

"So you knew about Grell?" Steve said.

"I was, as a matter of fact, approaching this problem from another direction when you came upon it in the way you did."

"But how. . . ?"

Dietrich interrupted. "As I told Fraulein Viner, others, as well as she, have an interest in seeing former Nazis punished. In such a town and in these circumstances, I can understand some suspicion. It is a pity. If Herr Viner had had confidence in me he would possibly be alive today."

"Then you know he is dead?"

"Of course," Dietrich said impatiently. "I did not know before but now I know that he was trying to establish that Josef Koll and the former SS Hauptsturmfuehrer were—or are—one and the same person."

He took a packet of Astors from his pocket and offered it to Steve. He lit both cigarettes and went on :

"Grell, whom I am now trying to find again, was involved in the murder of Fraulein Viner's father. He does not realize this. He was paid a quite large sum of money to impersonate Herr Viner, cross the border into West Berlin at Friedrich-strasse and recover his bag from the Ebert. If the murder became known, he would certainly be able to draw conclusions. However, as I understand, the identification of the body is difficult."

"That is far from the case. We are quite hopeful."

"Grell is not the only important link, of course. Somebody must have driven the car into East Berlin and also to Muggelsee and out again. It is an important line of inquiry."

Steve said : "Of course, it is not a line I have overlooked."

Dietrich smiled and said : "It is a most formidable task."

"That should be no deterrent."

"As far as I am concerned, it will not be."

Steve asked : "Why do you think it so formidable? I think it is certainly possible."

"If you were the police."

Dietrich paused to light a cigarette. Blowing out the flame he asked : "Have you begun such inquiries?"

Steve turned to face him.

"Now look here. I don't want to offend you but. . . . You've got me to come here and then you cross-examine me. I don't know who you are or what you represent and I have no reason at all to take you into my confidence. I want to start by asking you why you asked me to come."

Dietrich returned his gaze with wide, frank eyes and nodded.

"Your caution is reasonable. And on my side I have no way of convincing you of my good intentions. Please listen to me for a moment before I answer your question. It would be better if we go on walking."

After a few paces, he went on : "I start from the position that Mr. Viner was not murdered by anyone connected with any branch of intelligence work in Berlin. If any intelligence agency had been involved, they would have used the passport to get one of their own agents out and they would have handled the collection of the suitcase in a different manner. Grell as a minor member of the criminal classes fits into this picture perfectly.

"It is in these circles, the criminal classes, that we have to look for the other people involved and through them try to get back to the actual centre. Your own work must tell you that the best, possibly the only, way is through the criminal classes themselves. This is the kind of information that can be bought if you know where to buy it and can afford to pay."

He stopped talking for a moment and threw a look at Steve as though asking him to agree.

Steve said: "Go on," but it was clear that the man was not talking absolute nonsense.

"Very well," Dietrich continued. "It was such contacts that put me on the track of Grell and will possibly lead me to his new address. It is the same with the car-driver, or drivers. There were most probably several cars involved—each going over separately and the drivers meeting in East Berlin and using there probably one car only. This greatly widens the prospect of getting information. I feel sure that I shall be able to get this information without much more delay."

They were passing a waste bin and Dietrich carefully stubbed out his cigarette and put it inside.

"Now," he said. "You and Miss Viner are no longer under cover. The more you do, the more you will inform the opposition about what you are doing."

Impatiently, Steve put in: "I wish you would come to the point."

"Pardon. The point is to ask you and Miss Viner to stay out of action for a few days to give me time to pursue my own inquiries in the background. In a sense you would not be out of action but operating as a decoy. Or at any rate, giving the opposition something to do."

Seeing that Steve was about to speak, he went on: "One moment, please. The other matter is: if it becomes necessary to pay for information, may I take it that you would be able to share some of the costs, if necessary?"

"That's not the point," Steve said. "Yes, to that question if we have enough. On the other question; suppose you fail, we have lost time."

"Mr. Blake," the German spoke rather impatiently. "If I fail, I am sure you cannot succeed. I ask you to consider that."

After a long pause Steve sighed and said: "All right."

"Good. One question. Did the letters sent to someone by Mr. Viner ever come to light?"

On the point of saying Yes, Steve hesitated.

"Nothing, so far."

Dietrich looked surprised. "Then it was very clever of you to have found out about Koll being Kessel."

His expression made it very clear that he did not believe Steve. Let him think what he liked. Steve remained silent.

"I would stress, Mr. Blake, that if any such letters turn up, they should be kept in very safe keeping."

"Don't worry."

"One more thing. Since you are not any longer under cover, I would not recommend any trips to East Berlin until there is some development. You might detonate something if you try to cross."

"If you're unlucky and we too, the people in East Berlin anyway should know that Koll is Kessel." As an after-thought Steve added: "They should know about Grell, too."

Dietrich said gently: "At the cost of being indiscreet, I can assure you that what I know is known in East Berlin. Can we leave it at that?"

"I'll think it over," Steve said, resenting the one-sided conversation.

They had passed Teufelsee and were approaching the traffic of Heer Strasse.

"One necessary arrangement," Dietrich said. He gave the Englishman a piece of paper with a number typed on it. Steve noticed that he had worn gloves during their whole interview. "I know your number. I can get in touch if I need. Please pay attention. If you need to get in touch with me urgently, go to a call box and dial this number. Let the phone ring three times and break the connection. Repeat this twice. Three times three.

"Not long after, I shall telephone you from a public box. When you answer, I shall pretend it is a wrong number and say : *"Dass soll sechs sein."* Or maybe *"siebben"* and so on. This will mean that we should meet at the same place as today at six or seven, or whichever time is indicated in that way. You of course must take every care to be clean when you arrive. If you have a tail still at the indicated time, then do not come. Make it two hours later. Clear?"

Steve nodded. "But you may not be in when I ring."

"In these electronic days, Herr Blake, such things are the simplest to arrange."

He stopped and said : "We should part here."

Steve took the proffered hand.

"One hundred metres in that direction will bring you to Heer Strasse U-Bahn station. I shall get in touch with you as soon as possible."

He raised his hat and walked away.

Steve had been in over an hour when Mary came back after seeing the latest Sinatra private-eye thriller.

"I wish you were a private-eye," she whispered. "It makes everything so easy." She clung to him, relaxing slowly as he stroked her hair and soothed her.

"I've cooked your favourite dish while I waited—mutton cutlets with Roquefort cheese and baked potatoes."

She smiled wanly and kissed him.

"Tell me all about it."

So Dietrich knew about Koll being Kessel, and, if what he said was true, or what he hinted, the East Germans knew it too. And they hadn't published anything. So they must be working on it from another end.

"We should have taken those letters over there before this. And what about those fingerprints?" Mary looked worried. "And what did you think about Dietrich?"

"One thing at a time, my sweet. You may be right about the letters and now the prints but it's too late. We are under observation now and if he thinks he can get on the track of Grell in a day or two, I think we ought to play it his way till then. Lead normal-looking lives, go window shopping, see films, take long leisurely meals and go to bed in the afternoons. Let them waste their time."

"I don't like the situation," Mary said dubiously. "We're being passive. It's horrible wandering round like I did today, feeling all the time that I was being constantly watched. Any time we are out they could get in here and go over the place and find the letters and the fingerprints."

She watched Steve stroking his cheeks with his fingers and thumb, sticking out his lower lip, thinking.

"The letters are only copies," he said. "And Koll will always have his fingers. Let's give Dietrich two days."

Mary nodded. "But Steve, the letters and prints . . . I think you must keep them on you. You've got two breast pockets. Let's put them and the fingerprints in one pocket and stitch it up. Then they couldn't fall out or get taken by a pickpocket."

"O.K."

"And your gun. You shouldn't leave that around here either."

"I'll get a shoulder holster. I saw some in a shop near Bilka." He grinned. "Your personal 007, darling."

As Steve passed the big elm on the corner for the third time, Dietrich emerged apparently doing up his fly. They walked together in the direction of Teufelsee, Dietrich setting a smart pace. There was no greeting and no handshake.

"Two matters," Dietrich said without preamble. "One: I know where Grell is living. Two: I know who drove the car to Muggelsee. He is going under the name of Peter Schroeder. He is supposedly a taxi driver but that is peanuts. His real work is call-girls and marijuana. Like so many of his kind, he will take on any job that is not too dangerous and is well paid. A hire-car was used. That is to our advantage, though it was hired in another name."

It was exciting news. Steve said: "Now we seem really to be getting somewhere."

Dietrich said: "My idea is to get them both across to the other side."

"East Berlin?"

Dietrich nodded.

"Our adversaries are well organized," he went on. "In a case of this sort we should try to avoid a repetition of what happened to poor Singer. The best way to arrange that is to get them to where they can be properly protected."

"But," Steve began.

"Of course. They will not go willingly. This is why I need your help. In the first place with Grell. I shall be from the Federal Criminal Police. My papers are already prepared. The problem is your papers. You have to be from Scotland Yard. We shall arrest him and bring him to West Berlin. You may leave the rest to me."

The water, Steve felt, was getting deep.

"What have I to do?"

Dietrich answered: "You have to have a document which will pass at a pinch, for a German who knows no English, as a police pass. Have you a spare passport photo, available preferably without having to have it taken?"

Steve got out his press card, certifying his membership of the National Union of Journalists, Central London Branch.

"First class as it stands," Dietrich said. "All you need to do is go through a magazine and cut out the word 'police' in that size or so, and paste it over where it says press. He won't know what a real police document looks like. The words Central London are very impressive."

A couple came along toward them arm in arm and Dietrich stopped talking till they had passed.

"Grell," he said, "is in Frankfurt on Main. We shall meet there tomorrow at 22.00 hours—10 p.m. at this place."

He handed Steve a piece of paper with the name of two streets written on it.

"This is an intersection and there can be no confusion. Show it to a taxi driver. But only after you have taken exceptional care to see that you are clean."

Steve nodded.

"Then there is nothing more to discuss, unless you have something else."

"Nothing. Tomorrow evening at ten."

Dietrich nodded. "So now I must retire again to the bushes. I have a weak bladder."

He smiled at his own weak joke and slid into the bushes.

THIRTEEN

END OF THE SPOOR

STEVE arrived at Frankfurt Station with plenty of time to spare. Casting round in side streets within a small radius of the station he found a third-class hotel for twenty marks a night with a vacant single room. Behind a kind of restaurant bar, the proprietress sat stone-faced and constantly pursing her lips. A notice said: "No hot food after 3 p.m." Steve could not read it but when he saw what the few people were eating he dumped his bag in his room and went out.

Without being aware of it, he had landed in the prostitutes' quarter and almost every frontage in the nearby streets was some kind of joint. Their windows were filled with contorted photos of brass-faced women in various stages of undress.

How to make sure he had no tag? Most of the whores' customers seemed to be American occupation soldiers in mufti. It might be an idea. What G.I. ever knew a foreign language? Most of the girls would know a little English.

He paid and went out really scared for the first time in Germany. He had never in his life had anything to do with a prostitute. He walked round the block, sizing things up.

In a side street a tall, rather fat woman was standing in a doorway. He hesitated. Steve realized that in spite of his German hat he still did not look German, for she called softly:

"Wanna little love, darling?" Her accent anyway had been

learned from the international university for harlots—the U.S. army.

"I take you home, darling. Nice apartment. Whisky. Music. Good time."

"How much?" Steve asked.

"All night, 100 marks."

"Apartment, you said."

"Very nice."

"With back door?"

She looked wary. "Why you ask?"

"Back door?"

"Yes. It goes into back street. I don't want no trouble. You go, soldier."

She turned.

"No trouble." Steve felt in his pocket and brought out a 50-mark note.

"I go with you," he said, "and out of back door. You get this."

"I don' wanno trouble with police."

"Not police," he said. "Private."

"You be careful, Ami. I got a friend. No monkey business."

She led the way walking ahead into a darker street lined with shops, joints, hotels and pensions with notices for rooms. Next to a cheap bawdy house she turned into an entry and unlocked the street door, locking it after her.

Steve stopped her from pressing the illuminated button of the minute light. They stood in the half darkness.

"You wanna go now? Not come upstairs?"

He nodded, handed her a 50-mark note.

"Soldier," she said. "You on the run? AWOL? In trouble?"

Steve didn't know how to deal with that. Explanation would take too long and probably lead to misunderstanding.

"That's right."

"Na, good. You go."

She folded the 50-mark note and put it into Steve's pocket.

"You gonna need that."

"But. . . ."

She kissed him. It was a lovely kiss, moist and warm and friendly.

"Come," she said.

"Take the money," Steve said. "I've got more."

"You come see me sometime—another time."

Steve pulled the note out again.

"Don't make me angry, boy." She pulled his sleeve.

He followed her across the flagstones to another door and through a small entry.

Unlocking another street door and locking it again after them, she said: "That way. *Auf wiedersehen, liebling.* You come and see me?"

Steve nodded. He felt near to tears. He kissed her.

"Yes. *Auf wiedersehen.*"

He walked fast to the next well-lit street and a taxi was passing.

"Wohin?" asked the driver.

Steve had no idea. "Opera House," he ventured.

"OK, Buddy." The taxi driver switched to English.

At the opera house he jumped a passing tram, got out, walked through deserted streets, stopped at corners, turned back.

He was clean. That was sure. Another taxi took him to the corner of Breite Strasse and Wilhelm Strasse. There was still an hour to kill. But he was at the rendezvous, clean as a whistle, and could relax. Fifty yards from the corner was a small pub. It served hot food and he felt better for a plate of sauerbraten and several korns.

Almost on the hour he left the pub and walked to the corner. Dietrich arrived at the same moment.

"Let's walk," he said turning into a side street. "Grell is living a few minutes from here. I passed his house ten minutes ago and the light was on in his flat."

They walked in silence. Steve felt the tightening of his nerves and the exhilaration of the hunt. At last they seemed to be getting somewhere. From Grell the trail must lead back to Koll.

"Suppose he's not alone?" he remarked.

Dietrich shrugged his shoulders. "I'd thought of that. He doesn't know either of us. Best if I ring and make some enquiry about the family that used to live there. Name was Konradt. I saw it scratched out and his new name written over the top. He's calling himself Brenneisen. You can go one floor up and come down when I cough like this." He demonstrated.

"What about the taxi-driver?"

"I'll tell you later," Dietrich said in a curious tone. "We're here now."

They were in an old street of the kind that are declared condemned decades after ceasing to be worth repairing. It consisted entirely of ancient flats. Number 86 was entered through big wooden gates, now locked for the night and entered only by a postern. It led to one-time stables of a coal merchant. Inside was a dismal passage, big enough to take a horse-drawn coal cart on its cobbles and lit by a fly-blown yellow bulb. On each side was an opening leading to outworn stairs.

Dietrich led the way. He pushed a wall button and dirty light struggled through an insect filled globe. The stairs groaned and the banisters flapped. He stopped on the second floor and motioned Steve to go one higher. As Steve turned the next bend on the stairs he heard the pealing of an ancient pull-bell in the flat.

Nothing happened.

After a pause the distant clangour came again.

A minute passed and Steve heard Dietrich calling him quietly to come down.

He whispered: "He must be still out. Forgot the light. We'll go in and have a look round."

The stair light went out for the second time.

"Leave it," Dietrich whispered.

There was a noise of scraping and scratching going on for a minute. Dietrich once said: *"Scheisse!"* Then there was a click and the door opened. They both crept in and Dietrich gently closed the door on its snap lock. They were in a tiny corridor smelling of a dirty past, lit by a streak of light from a door standing ajar.

Dietrich took one pace and pushed open the door where the light was on with his hand round the lintel, taking no risks in the event that Grell was actually at home and waiting for them.

Well-trained, he crouched low and edged the side of his face round the door post—offering the smallest possible target in the least expected position.

"Herr Gott," he said and stood up.

Grell was at home.

He lay on his back across the crumpled bed. His head lolled over the edge, mouth open, gums showing. His upper denture lay on the floor. Wide eyes stared at nothing, upside down. There was a patch of red-brown on his shirt.

"Stay where you are," Dietrich told Steve. He went in and looked at the body. He did not touch it.

"Knifed," he said. "Let's get out of here fast."

Steve went on looking at the corpse, transfixed.

"Quick!"

"The passport," Steve said.

Dietrich gave a scornful laugh.

"We shan't find anything here."

He took out a handkerchief and wiped the door where he had touched it.

Going down the creaking stairs, Dietrich whispered: "There may be people watching this place. We must separate and make sure we haven't got any followers." He looked at his watch. "Meet me at midnight in a bar called the Wild West in Berliner Strasse near the station. If you sit at the bar I'll join you.

Dietrich was already sitting at the bar in the dusty-smelling joint. A floor show was in its stride—two women pretending to fight and pulling each others clothes off. They were getting advice from some drunken G.I.s.

Dietrich looked dejected. He ordered a whisky for Steve and stared blankly at the warring women on the floor.

"*Scheisse!*" he said suddenly. It appeared to be his favourite expression.

Steve said: "It's bad but it could be worse, I suppose. There's still the taxi driver, isn't there? You said you'd tell me about that."

Dietrich looked into his Scotch, then at Steve, then back. He poured the drink down and ordered two more.

"It's all here as a matter of fact," Dietrich said in a wan voice. He took his hand from his pocket and unfolded a piece of paper torn from the Berlin *Abend*.

The headline yelled: *"Taxi Fahrer Ermordet."*

"I can't read it," Steve said. "Can you translate it."

"Taxi driver murdered," Dietrich read. "Is the murder of

the taxi driver Peter Schroeder, only two weeks after Ernst Roth, the herald of a new series of killings for money?

"The Murder Commission does not think so. Their main reason is that last night's crime was clearly premeditated. It therefore does not fall into the category of casual killings to steal the night's takings from taxi drivers. This kind of murder has almost ceased since the installation of bullet-proof glass shields between the driver and passengers.

"In last night's case, according to the Murder Commission, careful preparations were made to entice the man out of the driver's seat. The murderer—it is thought that there must have been only one—was carrying a heavy case which had to be put in the boot.

"While Schroeder was either putting it in or getting it out he was stabbed through the right kidney. This well-known assassin's method of silent killing leads the police to believe that the killer was trained.

"The case, which was left behind, was found to contain bricks padded with newspapers."

"And so on," Dietrich said. He put the cutting away and sat staring moodily at his glass.

"That was the man who. . . ?" Steve began.

"He drove the killers in East Berlin on October 11. That was the man I was arranging to get across into East Berlin. Ptchah!"

Staring into the bar mirror, Steve saw that the girls had torn most of each other's clothes off and were finishing their turn by dancing together. He went on staring without seeing anything. Now there was almost nothing left to trace Viner's murderer. Singer, Grell, Schroeder, all dead. All killed as soon as their deaths had become necessary. As soon as he and Mary had got up close. They had wasted their time and only succeeded in getting one innocent man killed, one who was probably innocent and one who was almost certainly involved in the murder though not the actual killer. The killer was still untraceable, and the real killer, the organizer—Koll without question—was safe, safer than when they had started.

When he looked back he found Dietrich's eyes fixed on him, cold and hostile.

"I suppose even now you don't see what it means," Dietrich's voice was edged with contempt and cold anger.

Steve did not answer for some time and then said: "It certainly means we are further back than when we began."

"We!" Dietrich said bitterly. "We, my God!"

"Well, you tell me." Steve was getting angry too.

"Can't you see? It means that I'm blown too. Reduced overnight to nothing—useless—after years of building a cover and setting myself up. All ruined because I was stupid enough to try to correct your blunders. I should have stayed ten thousand miles away from your club-footed efforts at playing the detective. God, if only you had had the sense to stay out of it all and left it to us. Just given us the information. . . ." He shook his head helplessly. "No, no, we have to rush about, laying a trail like a swathe through a cornfield. Ach! What's the good?"

Steve sat silent, not even thinking, his brain numbed by the sudden onslaught.

"Two more whiskies," Dietrich ordered.

It was terrible whisky—about one-third Scotch and two-thirds low-grade vodka. When the two drinks arrived, Dietrich said quietly: "I'm sorry I exploded. This is a bad blow to me. I was well dug in here."

Steve still said nothing. He wanted to ask Dietrich how to go on from this point but the German's attack had robbed him of words and put him on the defensive.

Dietrich swilled his whisky round in the glass, making the ice clank, staring into it.

"In my profession, Mr. Blake, to be blown is bad enough. It is a sentence to what is, for an active man, living death behind a desk. I shall get a very small desk in view of the infantile failures I shall appear to have made. But that is a personal matter. What is, objectively worse, is that Koll is safer now than he was before Viner ever got on to him.

"And that itself is strange. Why, with so many Germans who were in Sachsenhausen, it took an Englishman to recognize him."

"It isn't a mystery," Steve said. "It was because of his English accent."

Dietrich stared at him incredulously.

"How do you know?"

Steve told him about the letters.

Dietrich groaned. "You've had them all this time? Oh, my God."

"Can you blame us for not trusting you?"

Dietrich remained silent, staring down, for a long time.

"No. I blame you rather for fancying you could get anywhere as an investigator. As in journalism, investigation is a profession which takes both flair and training. You should be the first to realize that. You should have left it to others."

"Such as whom?"

"Either to me, or since you did not trust me, to the people over there."

"In East Berlin?"

The other nodded.

"We didn't trust them either. That left only us."

Another long pause.

"Apart from saying how Viner spotted Koll, do the letters tell us anything else we don't know?"

"Nothing, really. A lot of detail which was fresh to him then and very convincing."

"They aren't very safe in West Berlin," Dietrich said.

"Those are copies," Steve reassured him, consciously refraining from touching the pocket where they were stitched into his suit. "The originals are still in London."

Dietrich nodded in apparent relief.

"I hope the solicitor won't lose them."

Steve did not answer.

"It's something," Dietrich went on. "Not much, but something. Disregarding the fact that you do not trust me," he held up a hand, "which I fully appreciate, I would most strongly advise you to get those letters to East Berlin as soon as you can. There really is not much left to do now but try to expose the man politically and in this, the letters would have some value. True, they would be shrugged off here as the fancies of a mentally deranged man, but they might lead to others coming forward and identifying Koll. There seems little chance left of pinning the Viner murder on him now. It would be hard enough on such a flimsy basis even to expose him as Kessel. But the letters are better than nothing."

Steve suddenly felt the desire to tell him about the fingerprints and was on the point of blurting it out when he stopped himself.

"I'll see that the copies get to East Berlin," he said.

"And make very sure that you aren't being followed before you cross the border," Dietrich said.

He paused a moment and added: "For my part, I shall not go back to West Berlin. It is far too dangerous. So this may be the last time we shall meet. Franz Dietrich has to submerge. I'm sorry that our short relationship was not as pleasant as it should have been, and also for my recent outburst."

He sighed. "Maybe I'll go to Vienna, change my identity and open a pastrycook's." He laughed and held out his hand.

Steve shook it. "Good-bye," he said and watched his back going.

He finished his whisky, wondering why he had suddenly decided not to tell Dietrich about the fingerprints. And then it occurred to him: Why hadn't Dietrich himself thought of the elementary idea of getting Koll's prints? Didn't he know that Kessel's prints were in the hands of the East Germans? He tried to work it out but he could no longer even pretend to think straight.

He got down from the high stool and was just going to leave when the barmaid pointed out that the bill was not paid. Always the sucker, me, Steve said to himself.

FOURTEEN

GINGLASS

MARY sat curled up in the corner of the big sofa, her face stiff with misery and frustration.

"What it comes to," Steve said, "is that we're a good local team playing the first division. We're outclassed in every direction we look."

He walked to the other end of the room and came back.

"For God's sake stop walking up and down."

"OK, darling." Steve flopped into a high-backed chair and felt for cigarettes.

"As far as connecting Koll with the murder of your father is concerned, they've blocked every way. There's nothing left at all to follow. They've been a jump ahead of us all the time. There's nothing left but your father's letters and Koll's fingerprints to connect Koll with Kessel, and nothing left at all to connect him with the murder."

Mary sniffed.

"You give up too easily," she said.

"I'd be happy if you would offer something a bit more positive." Steve walked over to the corner and poured a very big whisky.

"Leave that stuff alone," Mary said.

He looked round, grimaced and poured it back into the bottle.

"I feel as though we've been married for years," he said.

Mary lifted her head from her hands and tossed her hair back.

"You don't have to stick around."

"It just happens that hard as life might be with you, and I can see it isn't going to be a cakewalk, I simply cannot envisage it without you. I love you, Mary. It's the first time it has happened to me since I was eighteen and that doesn't count. I told you: wither thou goest and all that. But I'm only me. What do you want for your penny—Superman?"

Mary was already on his lap and kissing him. "I'm sorry, Steve, darling. I'm really sorry. I love you."

A few seconds later the phone rang.

Steve held Mary back, picked up the instrument, but did not speak.

There was a click and the line went dead.

He looked at Mary as he put it down. "They want to be sure we're at home."

Mary's eyes were scared. "What shall we do?" she whispered.

"Mary," he said, "I think Dietrich was right. There's one thing that has to be done. We must get that stuff to East Berlin. Now. At this moment."

"Then let's go."

"Not both of us."

"But I can't stay here alone," she wailed.

"It's very hard for two people to flush a tag. I've had more experience."

"You mean, you'd leave me here? No, Steve. I can't face it."

"Ssh, darling." He patted her cheek. "I've got an idea."

She waited miserably.

"Look, darling." He stopped. "Come over here."

He crossed the room and switched on the radio, tuning it to a station that was playing pop.

Into her ear, he said: "This place is very likely bugged. We should have thought of that before.

"My idea is this. I'll go out with you. Then we'll separate. I'll take evasive action and cross the border to give this stuff to Ginglass. In the meantime, you'll telephone Tempelhof—not from here—and book two seats on the first available plane after——" He looked at his watch—"five o'clock this afternoon. No, make it seven to allow enough time. Book indirectly if necessary. The main thing is to get out at once."

She nodded. "But. . . ."

"No buts. You take all the money but everything else we leave here. At Tempelhof, you leave my ticket with the customs—no, better—with the BEA. You will go straight into the waiting room, passing customs and immigration. Nothing can happen to you there. I'll join you there."

"But the flat? Our things?"

"Can't bother about that. I'll ring Scutts from London, or maybe the airport and pitch some tale. He'll manage."

"I want to be with you, Steve. I'm scared." She kissed him. "Just when we feel so sure of each other, darling."

"Work it out, Mary. It's the best way. By splitting up we stand the best chance to get that stuff over the border and by your making a phone booking and leaving the bags here, they will be led to think we aren't flitting. Come, darling. Don't let's waste time."

They got their coats. Steve left the radio on.

At the door he whispered. "I'd better not take this over the border. Shove it in your handbag."

She took the revolver gingerly and pushed it to the bottom of her big shoulder bag.

By seven o'clock it was clear that something had gone wrong. Their flight should be at seven-fifty. At seven o'clock she cancelled their bookings. She found a phone box where she could keep her eye on the hall through which Steve would have to come and telephoned the flat every quarter of an hour and listened to the ringing tone as it range into emptiness.

To go back alone to the flat was more than she could bring herself to do, but she could not spend the whole night at the airport. At ten she rang the Hotel am Zoo. They had a single room. She assumed that she was still being followed, so why not leave a message for Mr. Steven Blake saying where she had gone?

At the hotel she dialled the flat again. No answer. Then Jack Scutt's home number but put the receiver down before he could answer. He could scarcely help and why drag him into such a mess?

The big question was: had Steve been detained in East Berlin or in West Berlin? Mentally she skirted round any other possibility and kept all thought of Singer and Grell at bay. Without logical reason, as she herself felt, her suspicions of the East Germans grew. The real enemy must be Koll. But her father had been murdered in East Berlin. If, knowing what she knew, she had such suspicions, nobody in the West would doubt for a moment that he had been murdered by "the Communists." That was where Koll had been so bloody clever.

She could visualize the headlines—"Viner—A Double-Agent?"; "How was Viner Decoyed to Muggelsee?"; "Why the Reds Could Not Let Sachsenhausen Man Live." They could write whatever they pleased about a dead man but Koll was alive and rich and well able to take legal action against any newspaper that published a single word it could not prove in court.

She fell asleep without undressing. Later she surveyed the

ruins of her frock and washed it, using ordinary soap, and got into bed.

In the morning she phoned the flat again. Tears came into her eyes as she remembered Steve's advice for a morning pick-me-up. She rang the waiter and ordered breakfast—cold chicken and half a bottle of champagne. He raised his eyebrows.

"Sekt?"

"No, not sekt. Champagne. What have you?"

He fetched the wine list. She chose a Bollinger.

After it she felt better able to think.

There always seemed to be only one thing to do and that seemed always to turn out wrong. But she could see no alternative to going to East Berlin and seeing Ginglass. If Steve had gone there and was being held—well, why shouldn't she be in the same boat? If not she would at least know that he was in West Berlin, if he was still. . . . She blocked that thought.

Her room looked out over Kurfürstendamm and a passing bus gave her an idea. She paid another night in advance—having no baggage—and strolled out of the hotel, turned left and crossed the road, slowly window shopping. Opposite the Memorial Church a placard advertised times and routes of Berlin Sightseeing Tours which took trippers to East Berlin. Without stopping she took it in as she went by. A bus would be leaving at 10.30 to visit Unter den Linden, Alexander-platz, Treptow, Koepenick with half an hour stop at the Berolina Hotel for refreshments. She sauntered on and let the clock get round to 10.25 before slowly idling back. Opposite the bus stop, she stared into the window of a hand-bag shop.

Considering that the bus was half-empty the conductor's calls that there was room for a few more seemed unnecessary.

She waited till he climbed on board and walked over to it rapidly and got in.

"Just in time," he said. "Fifteen marks please."

The doors shut with a hiss. Nobody had got in after herself. From the empty back row she saw that nearly all her fellow-passengers were Japanese—a tourist group obviously. There were a few American army men in their super-pressed and badly fitted uniforms, accompanied by nasal-voiced women. In front of her a U.S. sergeant reassured his wife: "It's Okay, honey. Nothing ever happens on these trips."

Mary sat listening to the bored loudspeaker voice making announcements in a kind of English and waiting only for the arrival at the Berolina.

On the way back from Lichtenberg the black Opel Kapitan pushed itself into her consciousness. She went forward to an empty seat from which she could watch it in the driving mirror. It fell behind on open stretches, pulled closer at crossings. It had nothing to worry about. The bus route was scheduled. She had not dropped them after all.

While her fellow passengers bought beer, coffee and post-cards in the big glass foyer, Mary ran up to the mezzanine floor, dialled the Attorney General's office and asked for Dr. Ginglass.

"Sekretariat, Dr. Ginglass," a woman said. No. Dr. Ginglass was in conference. Impossible to reach. Mary just stopped her from ringing off.

"This is a murder case," she said. "Miss Viner from London. I must speak to him at once."

"Oh, Miss Viner! One moment."

Three or four minutes passed. She had to go out with the bus if she was to pass back through the border.

"Ginglass," said the phone. "Where are you, Miss Viner?"

She told him.

"I will come."

"The bus leaves in fifteen minutes."

"Never mind."

She walked down into the foyer and got herself a big brandy and a coffee. The minutes ticked round on the wall clock. The Japanese and Americans gathered up their coats and handbags and strolled to the automatic doors.

A girl came to Mary and said: "Come this way, please."

Ginglass was waiting in a small reception room.

"We wondered when you would get in touch, Fraulein Viner."

"The bus has to leave," she said. "So I can't stay. I came this way because I was being followed—and still am. Did Mr. Blake come to see you yesterday?" He shook his head. "We'll talk later."

Plump and humourless he might be, but Ginglass now showed an unexpected ability to take decisions. He had the bus driver sent in and told him that the lady wished to stay a little longer in East Berlin, gave him his visiting card and said he would telephone the border police at Checkpoint Charlie to explain.

He did that next and then told Mary: "After we have had a chat I will arrange for you to go back another way if you wish. Personally, I don't think you should return to West Berlin at all. Now let us go to lunch."

Mary shrugged her shoulders mentally and decided that it was not possible to hurry the man. She felt lucky to have got so far.

Lunch turned out to be at the Ganymed, East Berlin's poshest restaurant next to the Berthold Brecht theatre, where the waiters wear tailsuits and often sport party badges. Mary had no fault to find with the roast knuckle of veal, nor with the wine.

At the first moment, she repeated her question, knowing the answer.

"Did Mr. Blake come to see you yesterday?"

"No."

"Maybe he sent you something."

Ginglass shook his head. "What kind of something?"

"Some photo copies of my father's letters and some finger-prints."

"Fingerprints?"

"Koll's."

"Josef Koll?" His eyebrows went up.

"Yes."

"Would you mind explaining."

"But you know."

"I'm sorry. I don't know what you are talking about."

Mary said: "But you already know that Koll is Kessel."

"How should I? Assuming that it is so."

Mary thought back over what Steve had told her. But if the East Germans did not know that Koll was Kessel, how did Dietrich know?

"But Dietrich said that the people here knew," she said.

"And who is Dietrich?"

She told him. He listened quietly sometimes shaking his head.

"So, Fraulein Viner," he said, "at the expense of seeming impolite, I must say that you and Mr. Blake have not helped by your activities but rather the contrary. Although your father was only able to recognize Koll because of his curious English accent, there is no doubt that it was only a matter of time before we had traced the whole thing to Koll, coming from the other direction, via the murderers."

He studied his fingernails and went on: "It was most exasperating for our people. They had to avoid contacting

F

you after the death of Singer because you were both under observation. And then, when at last it seemed imperative to warn you, it was too late. With Grell and Schroeder gone, we have to start all over again. If you had contented yourselves with giving us the letters, we could have done the rest in such a manner that Koll could be brought to account for the murder of your father. That is much more important than proving he was Kessel. For your father's murder he could get twenty years and the case would incidentally prove that he was the former SS guard Kessel. Merely for being Kessel he simply would not be put on trial at all in these days when Hitler's swivel-chair murderers are amnestied unless you can prove malice." He laughed bitterly. "Mass murder without malice! It's a new concept of law.

"And now it seems most unlikely that we shall ever be able to prove a case of murder against him. That is not certain, of course. There must have been one other accomplice in the actual killing, possibly even two. We shall still continue our work on those lines. I shall of course give instructions for Koll's fingerprints to be obtained. In the last case, if all fails, we may only have left the weapon of public denunciation. Not much but better than nothing."

He took a sip of wine and sat silent.

"We did not come over because we did not trust you. Mr. Blake thought you might publish the facts before the time was ripe."

He smiled sadly. "That is enough about that. We can't reverse the past. Let us at least have an understanding about our next steps.

"You mentioned that the letters of your father were copies. You still have the originals safely?"

"Yes. They are. . . ."

He held up a plump hand. "I don't need to know where

they are. It would be useful if you would arrange for me to have copies of them as soon as possible. Can you do that?"

Mary nodded.

"Since they are in any case only copies, you could have them air-freighted to yourself, care of this office. If they were put on a Polish direct flight as air-freight there is no danger of their being intercepted."

"I understand," Mary said.

"And now, this man Dietrich. Are you still in contact with him?"

"No. In Frankfurt he told Mr. Blake that his work in West Germany and West Berlin had been ruined and he had to disappear."

Ginglass nodded thoughtfully.

"Curious how much he seems to know."

"About Koll, you mean?"

"Not only. Also about the others—Singer, Grell and Schroeder. Please describe him to me."

He made rapid notes as Mary drew a verbal portrait of Dietrich.

He paid the waiter.

"Fraulein Viner," he said, "I don't think you should go back to West Berlin."

"But I must."

"It is most unwise. I think you will be in danger."

"There is nothing else I can do. I can't just leave Steve— Mr. Blake—not knowing what has happened. After all, they've got what they want—the letters and the fingerprints."

"They only have the copies of the letters."

Mary looked up.

"I see what you mean. I will telephone London tonight and have the copies sent and arrange for the originals to be put in a safe deposit."

"But do not telephone from your flat."

"Oh! No. I will do it outside."

"Let me advise you again not to go back to West Berlin. Let us do the work. We have better means."

"I must. Perhaps Steve—Mr. Blake—is already back at the flat."

He sighed. "I understand your feelings. If you are quite determined, I will arrange for you to be passed through the border."

He gave her his card, scribbling an extra number on it.

"My private number. Please keep us informed."

Outside he said: "One more thing, Fraulein Viner. While a possibility still exists of proving the murder of Herr Viner against Koll, it would be as well if you gave us permission to continue to preserve your father's remains. After, we shall have to see what happens."

Mary nodded, unable to speak.

As he left her at Friedrichstrasse S-Bahn station he said: "Please take every care."

At Zoo station she called the flat. No answer. And no answer from Scutts' office either. She remembered, he had to go to Bonn.

She had never felt so lonely.

FIFTEEN

NEWS OF BLAKE

BACK in the hotel she had a long cry and felt calmer but completely at a loss what to do next.

Then she remembered the letters. Her promise to Ginglass.

She looked at her watch. Four-fifteen. What time did solicitors close their offices? Very early, no doubt.

"There is at least an hour's delay on London calls," Long Distance told her.

Leave it till tomorrow? No. Solicitors certainly did not get to their offices till after ten. It would tie her down.

"Is there an urgent service?"

"Yes, madam. Twice the normal charge. But there may be other urgents waiting. It could take almost as long. Blitz is immediate."

"And costs."

"Five times the normal charge."

"Blitz it then, please."

Almost at once she was talking to Goldfield's secretary.

"Mr. Goldfield is at this moment leaving."

"Can't you stop him. I'm phoning from Berlin."

It took several minutes—money ticking away—and she heard Goldfield's plummy voice, panting.

"Miss Viner. Pardon my breathlessness. I came back up the stairs. No lifts in these old buildings."

"I'm sorry."

"Not at all. Not at all. What can I do for you?"

"It's about my father's letters. . . ."

"That's all in order, Miss Viner. Quite all right. I have carried out your instructions."

"My instructions?"

He caught the questioning note. "Yes, Miss Viner. Your letter. I gave your messenger the documents as you instructed. Against his signed receipt, of course."

"My God," Mary wailed.

"Is something wrong?"

"What did you give him?"

"What you instructed: your father's letters from Germany and the handwritten manuscript."

After a speechless pause Mary said again: "Oh, my God!"

"What is wrong, Miss Viner?"

"I sent no letter."

Now the pause came at his end.

"But I assure you. . . . The letter was on your own headed notepaper, typed of course, but on the Flask Avenue paper and with your signature. I took the precaution of comparing it with one here which I knew to be genuine. I sincerely hope that nothing has gone wrong."

"Nothing gone wrong!" She was shouting. "Nothing wrong! You idiot. I. . . ." She stopped. "I'm sorry."

She put the receiver down.

There was nothing left now. No letters. No fingerprints. No witnesses and no Steve.

Hopefully she tried to think that now they had all the evidence they would let Steve go. But that was clearly absurd. Steve still constituted a witness. Why should such people show any mercy if it added to their danger? With all their resources what would be easier than to dispose of an unknown, unimportant and undesirable witness?

But all those arguments applied to her as well. She was no less dangerous to them than Steve.

There was still no answer from the flat.

But she had to eat. Down in the hotel restaurant she sat at a table reserved for hotel guests, eating slowly to pass the time.

It was a brilliant cold morning. Full of ham and eggs, Mary spent two hours on S-Bahn, U-Bahn, buses, taxis and walking in side streets. She saw no signs of anyone following her. Making sure she had plently of small change she took a taxi to the flat and had paid the driver almost before it stopped.

As she turned to go in, her eye seemed to catch the movement of a curtain in a window over the road. It would, she now realized, be the obvious thing to do. To put a watcher there. But on the other hand, it might not be Them at all. The Germans were the most neighbour-conscious people in the world, performing much of their overt action for the benefit of the neighbours and much of the rest of their waking hours observing whether the neighbours were behaving themselves.

It took her a few minutes to pluck up the courage to go up the stairs to the flat floor. Just in case Steve were there, she rang the bell. Nobody came to the door.

Suddenly making up her mind, she pushed the key in and turned it. A heavy Japanese vase inside the door, used as an umbrella stand, was handy to prop the door wide open.

Drawing a deep breath she pushed open the living-room door. It was as she had left it. Leaving all doors open as she went she toured the flat. It was empty. No Steve. No message.

With the front door closed, deadlocked and chained, she sat

in the sunshine in the living-room with a whisky and a cigarette.

Lying half awake all night, her brain had gone on working, endlessly going over the same ground. Go to the police. Useless. The British authorities? Useless. First though, she must try to find out whether the British consul had been contacted in any way about Steve. Next, to find out whether a body answering his description had been reported. For that, she would have to start by going to the police in any case.

And supposing that whatever had happened to Steve should happen next to her. The trail would end entirely. A letter to her paper saying what had happened? No. To the Consul? No. Scutts?

Well he was a newspaperman. It was a story he could try to take up. Someone would know, at least.

She got paper and a ballpoint, thinking: Good God, I'm doing just the same as Daddy did. She started "Dear Jack" and wrote steadily and concisely for ten minutes or more, telling him all the main facts. When she had finished, the thought struck her that maybe Steve had suddenly had to go somewhere and would also turn up, cheerful as ever. It was a stupid notion but it gave her the idea of writing to him as well.

"Darling Steve, I don't know whether you will ever read this but I feel so lonely and don't know which way to turn now. Everything we have touched seems to have gone wrong. And you don't know what it's like, wondering what has happened to you. Of course, Koll is behind it, as always. He seems to be able to do whatever he likes. I feel that at any time now, I shall be the next. I don't want to live without you anyway. I love you so much, Steve my dear, sweet, elderly, fat darling.

I can't leave Berlin without you, Steve, and I can't leave Berlin unless I have done everything I can to punish Koll. I have not had it out of my mind since I first knew what really must have happened to my mother. Maybe, because you aren't a woman you can't understand what it means to me. I suppose I'll never know who my real father is, so that I could personally kill him. But Koll I know and I can't live in the same world as him. I've had all kinds of wild ideas about going to confront Koll, attacking him in public and getting arrested, anything, just to do something and not wait passively always for him to move in his own time. Darling Steve, I try to stop myself thinking that they have killed you too, but I can't see why they haven't. Good-bye, my darling, I love you."

Mary put this in an envelope addressed it "Steve Blake, Private" and sealed it with tape, put it and the letter to Scutts into another envelope and sealed that too. Then she wrote a brief note to Scutts: "Dear Jack, If I don't call and collect the enclosed by three o'clock on Friday afternoon, please open it and take whatever action you think fit." It was Wednesday. Two days should be enough.

She was looking up the number of the British consul when the phone rang. She stood irresolute as it went on ringing and stopped, leaving its noise in the room. She cursed herself for not answering. Perhaps Steve had been ringing the flat as she had been. She went and stood by the phone.

It gave a little hiccup and rang again.

She picked it up at once and said: "Hallo."

There was a click and the line went dead.

She stood holding the phone, chilled. They wanted to find out if she was there. Slowly she put it down and then hastily picked up her handbag and coat. She must get out.

She unlocked the front door, slid the chain out and opened the door and drew back with an audible gasp of indrawn breath.

The man who stood there took off his hat. It was Dietrich.

"I was just going to ring," he said.

Mary stepped back, staring at him, and pushed the letter into her overcoat pocket. He followed her in, holding his forefinger to his lips, and shut the door.

"Bathroom." He did not speak but formed his mouth so that she could lip-read.

Mary had a half-hysterical desire to laugh. He surely hadn't come dying to have a pee?

She led the way, showed him the bathroom door and turned to go. He started turning on the taps and beckoned her inside.

Through the rush of water he said: "This place must be bugged in every room, I imagine."

"What are you doing in Berlin?" Mary asked. "You told Steve. . . ."

He held up a hand to stop her. "I shouldn't be in Berlin at all. I had to come. In fact I'm here because of Mr. Blake."

"Where is he?" She sat down on the edge of the bath, weak at the knees with relief.

"Quite close."

"Is he all right?"

He nodded. "I kept telephoning here. No answer. I had to come, stupid though it was to run the risk. Mr. Blake is worried about you."

"I simply don't believe you."

He turned his large blue eyes to her.

"I'm sorry about that," was all he said.

For some time the only sound was of the water rushing.

"I went to East Berlin yesterday."

He raised an eyebrow. "And?"

"They don't know you there."

He smiled.

"Don't you think you are being a little naïve, Miss Viner? Of course they don't know me there. Nobody in public life ever admits the existence of special agents. Still, they exist."

He took out a packet of Astors and offered her one.

"Well," she said, "why have you come?"

"To take you to Mr. Blake. After that. . . ." He shrugged his shoulders. "After that, I don't know."

"Have you seen Steve?"

"Not since Frankfurt."

"Then how do you know where he is?"

He made a gesture of despair with his hands.

"The only question is whether you want me to take you to him."

"How do I know that this isn't a trap?"

"You cannot know that, if your own logic doesn't tell you. But I warn you that this may be the last chance of getting you and him out of West Berlin. And even that I cannot promise you."

She sat still for a long time, listening to the water.

"I'll come," she said.

He turned the taps off. She opened her mouth to say something but he shook his head.

Mary picked up her gloves and bag and followed him out of the flat.

Downstairs he said: "Wait here till you see my car pull up outside and then come in. No talking please. I have to give all my attention to seeing that we are not tailed. It is much harder in a car."

It was a hired sports car. Dietrich drove it expertly making use of every opportunity. Mary was glad of the chance not to talk, to day-dream about meeting Steve, plump, untidy Steve. When the car stopped she thought it was traffic lights again but Dietrich said: "We're there."

He had stopped the car in a drive at the side of a large house standing in beautifully tended gardens within a high wall. Steel rods set in the stonework protected the basement windows. She followed him round to the back and down a few steps to a door—a kind of servants' entrance, it seemed, because there were french windows at ground level, opening on to a terrace.

He led the way along a passage and opened a door on the right, standing aside for her to enter. She stepped in and the door closed behind her. Turning back she saw the door handle latch up and heard a bolt slide.

"Hey! Let me out!" she yelled, twisting and pulling the handle.

The heavy door did not move and there was no sound from the other side.

She was in a large windowless cellar, unheated and used as a store. Two walls were covered with shelves full of packages and tinned goods. Another wall was lined with bottle racks, filled with bottles. Small cast-iron ventilators were set high under the ceiling.

She picked up a tin of some kind and banged on the door, shouting till she grew hoarse. Furious she picked out a bottle and hurled it at the door. She followed it with another and another and a heap of broken glass and a pool of liquor grew. Feeling herself getting dizzy from the alcohol fumes she stopped, panting with rage.

Twenty minutes passed. There was nothing she could do and she was hungry. She made a good meal of Russian black caviar, water biscuits, potted partridge and champagne.

The bolt clicked back and there was a scratching and chinking of glass as the door was pushed open a few inches against the pile of smashed bottles.

Dietrich put his head round the door, taking in the damage.

"Come in," Mary said. "Come in, you treacherous swine, if you dare."

He dodged back as a bottle of claret smashed on the wall near his head.

"Fraulein Viner," he called through an inch-wide crack. Mary pulled another bottle from the rack and swung it, ready to launch it at his head.

"Fraulein Viner. Listen please. I have a message for you."
She waited.

"What is it, you piece of offal?"

"It is from Herr Koll. He wishes to see you."

"Your fascist boss. Where is Steve Blake?"

"Herr Koll will no doubt tell you. The matter is out of my hands."

After all, to meet Koll had been one of her aims and it would make no difference now whether she acquiesced or not. But she had left no messages. Nobody knew she had come here. Tricked at every move; out-planned and out-manoeuvred.

"Where is Koll?"

"Upstairs in his study. I can take you to him at once."

"All right. I'll go."

Dietrich pushed the door slowly open, shifting the sludge of smashed glass and liquor. His eyes did not meet hers but wandered round the shambles she had created to pass the time and do what little harm she could. Champagne bottles stood in rows with their corks out, pots of caviar and costly imported foods lay smashed in a corner: the things for which people lied, cheated and murdered. Mary watched him as he took it in and on her way to the door picked up a bottle of French cognac and dropped it on the stone floor.

"Which way, you creep?" she asked. "Where is your owner?"

He pointed the way up a flight of stairs topped by a padded door which opened into the entrance hall of the house.

It was large and high-ceilinged, surrounded by ancestral-style paintings varnished down to burnt umber through which some highlights struggled. They were all in heavy gold frames dripping with fern-fronds and acanthus. A marble stairway led up to a gallery running round a vast cut-glass chandelier. Everything was in keeping—gilt, ormolu, brocade —everything screamed of wealth and lack of taste.

As they mounted the marble stairs, Mary felt her own heart beating. She had strained every nerve after this man for weeks and now she was to meet him. She did not want to. She had no idea what to say or do. Must keep calm. Breathe deeply. A showdown with Koll was what she had to have and now she was going to meet him. He had arranged it. It showed that he was scared of her. Let him talk. The fear went and she felt calm, even exhilarated.

A door opened into a totally different atmosphere, as quiet and tasteful as the entry had been garish and vulgar. Dark wood, deep carpet, hidden lighting, a few pieces of charming furniture.

Dietrich crossed a large lounge, opened a door and motioned her in, standing aside and shutting the door after her. She gathered her nerves for the meeting.

She was alone.

It was a large, comfortable room lined with books and dark natural wood. On the windowless side a wood fire burned in a big open fireplace of dark red-brick, flanked by leather arm-chairs. At the end was a large desk with nothing on it but two telephones. She sat on the arm of a chair and lit a cigarette.

For a moment she thought of using the telephone. But Scutts was away and she did not know the number of the consulate.

It was too late anyway. The door opened and Koll walked in.

SIXTEEN

AT BAY

KOLL shut the door without turning round, his hand behind him. She heard the key turn but he did not take it out of the lock.

He gave her a little bow. "Koll," he said in introduction but did not offer his hand. He was wearing very thin black leather gloves and smiled as he caught her glance at them.

Walking with the grace of a cat, he passed her and stood behind the desk. His clothes had the ease and careless fit that only the most expensive tailors achieve.

"Please take a seat," he said.

She studied his face, looking for the mark of the murderer, torturer, sadist. Steve had judged him badly, but he was only a man. No woman would trust that face for an instant. The blue eyes were bright and quick but expressionless—stone—for all that small wrinkles round them lent them a false bonhomie. But it was the mouth, full and soft, that gave him most away. She could feel his warped sexuality. He was about to enjoy himself, not because she was a woman but because she was a human victim.

She stopped herself from demanding to know where Steve was.

"How do you feel," she said conversationally, "when people die and can't suffer any more. Do you feel cheated? Do you feel sorry for yourself? A kind of post-coital triste?"

"Would you care to sit down?" he said, as though she had not spoken.

"Of course," she said, "you are a sick man. I suppose that when you were a Hauptsturmfuehrer in Sachsenhausen, nobody noticed that you were crazy and now you have so much wealth and power that nobody dares to tell you that you really should be in a madhouse."

She sat down on the arm of a chair. Koll took his seat behind the desk. He continued to look at her without change of expression.

"And now," she said. "What next?"

"I regret the way I had to arrange this meeting. . . ."

She laughed. "Suppose we cut out the phoney gentleman stuff. OK. You had me decoyed here. In any case I was coming."

"I was a little surprised that you had not got in touch before. There are obviously a few matters to be cleared up."

"I think you ought to know that if I don't reappear the British authorities will know where I am."

He raised one corner of his lips a millimetre in a tiny smile.

"Fraulein Viner. First, I assure you that I have no intention of detaining you. But also I do not think you have informed the British. As I understand, you had a letter in your hand which I suggest would be found in your pocket or handbag at this moment."

Mary hesitated before saying: "Think what you will."

It sounded lame. Her own foolishness had lost her ground. Her claim to have written to the British was evidence of fear. And fear was what he liked. No doubt he could smell it, like an animal. She sat and waited.

Koll opened a drawer and took out a silver cigarette box which he pushed across the table top.

"Please smoke if you wish."

"I'll smoke my own. I asked you: what next?"

"That depends on what you decide after I have made the situation clear."

"Before I listen to anything, I want to know about Mr. Blake."

He let her wait until he had taken a cigarette and lit it carefully.

"Herr Blake is well. Still suffering very mildly from a blow on the head which he seems to have received shortly before he arrived. He has, of course, no longer some photostat copies of letters supposedly written by your father. Nor has he the fingerprints of some unidentified person which were with the letters. He appeared to have lost them in some fracas in which he also received the blow on his head."

He looked at his gloved hands.

"Who could believe a word you say?"

He waved his cigarette deprecatingly. "I assure you that nothing has happened to Herr Blake. If only to ensure a greater degree of confidence between us, I will prove it to you."

He picked up one of the phones and pressed a button.

"204," he said.

"Hallo. Put the Englishman on the line."

He held the phone out. Mary crossed the carpet, took it and wiped the earpiece with her sleeve.

"Hallo!" It was Steve's voice.

"Darling," Mary realized too late that this was also a mistake. "Steve, are you all right?"

"Mary. How did you get through? Where are you?"

"I'm. . . ."

Koll pressed a gloved finger on the telephone rest and the call was cut off.

"You see," he said.

Mary went back to the arm of her chair.

Koll went on : "Those letters do not exist any more, either the originals or the copies. Your father is not in a position to write any more letters or to try to establish, as he seemed to believe, that Josef Koll was once someone else. On the contrary, as I understand, it is very unlikely that there will ever be proof that Herr Viner is not alive and well, somewhere."

Mary felt herself shaking as the insolent, confident voice went on. She gripped her hands in her lap and kept herself from saying anything.

"Owing to the carelessness of some of my people in allowing you to cross to East Berlin yesterday—which they had specific instructions to prevent——"

"What will you do to them?" Mary broke in. "Have them broken on the wheel or crucified on an ant hill?"

"You may safely leave such matters to me." He smiled. "As I was saying : it is now possible that the East Germans suffer under the same delusions. If so they may try to make a fuss. That is nothing to worry about as far as I am concerned. They have not a shred of evidence in their possession.

"Any unsubstantiated charge such as the East Germans could now bring in the case of Josef Koll would be immaterial. Any antipathy it caused would be counterbalanced by sympathy and even prestige—which I scarcely need."

"Considering all of which," Mary said, "you seem to be going to a lot of trouble."

Koll nodded. "I intend to be very frank with you. Such frankness is necessary if you are to understand the situation and so make a sensible choice."

He sat for a moment and went on : "It would be folly for me to deny that this business has overtones. It involves a British prisoner in Sachenhausen. There is the fact that my head office is in the British occupation zone in West Berlin. There is, even more important, the fact that it is now common knowledge that my holdings are the decisive ones concerned with developing the British, Dutch, German consortium for the gas-centrifuge production of enriched uranium. The matter had a sensational quality best avoided."

"And still has," Mary said.

"To a much more limited extent than before. You, for example, never met the person that I was imagined by Herr Viner to have been. Being his daughter does not make you a witness. On the contrary it would be thought that you supported your father's mistaken beliefs out of filial loyalty."

He took another cigarette and tapped it carefully, blowing the end before putting it to his lips. He smoked Players.

"Fraulein Viner, you are a newspaper woman. You know what happened in the Speidel case. General Speidel was a person who would be without question regarded as what is described as a war criminal. But it did not prevent him from winning a libel action against a British film company. Do you think that any British newspaper would dare to publish what you could tell them, or what the East Germans could tell them, knowing that they would face legal action by a man with the wealth to carry it to the end? Not to mention that your Foreign Office would be most annoyed—when it has worked so hard to develop our good relations. No. No."

Mary inwardly agreed. Her own paper would not touch the story as it stood.

"You seem to be going to inordinate lengths if the matter is so insignificant," she said, though it was hard to keep her voice steady.

He folded his gloved hands together and rested his chin on them. The essence of patient reasonableness.

"I don't think it is necessary to explain that there is a difference between being able to surmount a problem and avoiding it either entirely or mainly. I have excellent reasons for avoiding such an affair at this time. Germany is on the eve of great developments. For long enough there has been a disparity—Herr Strauss it was who said that West Germany was an economic giant but a political dwarf. That situation is now rapidly changing, and not a little due to the active help of your own Foreign Office."

He patted the desk top with his gloved fingertips. "You do not need to be told that the enterprises which I lead are playing a major role in these developments. Clearly I am ready to go to extreme lengths to avoid diversionary matters which could harm the progress of my country."

Mary tossed her hair back and laughed. "You're crazy," she said. "And I am waiting for the answer to my question."

"Your question?"

"Yes. What happens next? I did not need to come here for a political speech. I can get that from von Thadden, far better too."

"Pff," he snorted. "Those people. Foot soldiers."

He flicked his cigarette and Mary noticed the gesture described by her father. "Well then, what next?"

"On grounds of expediency, the simplest solution is not necessarily the best. By that I mean the solution of having you and your lover Blake eliminated. There might be some echo."

"There would be. But it is very considerate of you just the same."

"Expedient. I am not sentimental."

Mary laughed scornfully. "Not sentimental. My God. After all that Volkisch twaddle about the rising greatness of the twice-defeated imperial German fatherland. Der Tag and all that. Sentimental tripe."

"As you please. So let me say that I prefer to reduce the possibility of trouble."

"And how will that be?"

"You will sign a document saying that you are convinced that your father was suffering from delusions in confusing Josef Koll with the former Hauptsturmfuehrer Kessel. The document would not be used, of course, unless you or your comrades in East Germany forced me to produce it. You would of course let them know of its existence."

Mary reacted instantly. "You can go to hell," she said, keeping her voice low. "You are and will always be Herr Hauptsturmfuehrer Kessel. You schizophrenic Nazi sub-man."

Koll sat still, smiling.

"Actually," he said, "you should realize that these insults are the only weapons you have and that is why you employ them. But seen objectively, my offer is magnanimous. There are other ways of dealing with the affair, much less pleasant for you, much more trouble for me, but in fact more effective."

He rested his hands on the table top, very calmly, watching her. A jet plane went over from Tempelhof. Mary wished she were on it, sitting next to Steve.

"Perhaps you would be more easily convinced if I told you of the third possibility."

"Third?"

"Yes. Elimination, a statement signed by you and," he ticked them off on his fingers, "a third. As you know, Scotland Yard inquired about Herr Viner. I happen to know the content of the report that went back from the West Berlin police. Herr Staengel, the chief of detectives, is a friend of mine, a very good friend."

"What was his line?" Mary asked savagely. "Pulling out fingernails, strangling babies or making lampshades from human skin?"

Koll smiled again. "Herr Staengel reported to your police that Herr Viner had been under observation for some time by the West German counter-intelligence. It was suspected that he was engaged in espionage for the East Germans. The most likely explanation for his disappearance was that, realizing he was suspected, he was withdrawn and allowed to 'disappear' behind what Dr. Goebbels described as the Iron Curtain—an expression taken over by Winston Churchill as his own invention."

He paused and smiled again.

"It would be assumed," he said, "that East Germans warned him that he was being followed and sent someone else over the border using his passport to collect his baggage. A very ingenious double play. At all events, he disappeared."

Mary fought for control. It was filthy to watch this sadist enjoying himself.

"You organized it very well," she said. "It was Dietrich who actually killed my father, wasn't it?"

Without answering, Koll went on: "Now we come to the fact that both you and Herr Blake have visited East Berlin—who knows how many times?"

He opened a drawer and took something out.

"Perhaps you would like to see these."

Mary did not move.

"Well, never mind. I will tell you what they are and you may see them if you doubt my word. This is a photograph showing Herr Blake entering the headquarters of the East German Communist Party."

Mary corrected him: "Socialist Unity Party."

"As you will. Why split hairs? This is one showing Herr Blake apparently handing something to someone in East Berlin. There is no doubt where it is, you can see the Brecht theatre in the background."

He picked up the third, slowly.

"This is an excellent one, though the quality could be better.

It was taken on ultra-fast film without flash but it is good enough. It shows yourself sitting in a night bar which is, I am told, readily identifiable as the Linden Corse in East Berlin. There is a bottle of wine on the table and you are showing something to a man who is a well-known Communist and very much concerned with several sorts of questionable activities."

Mary said : "So what?" but she was beginning to feel cold inside. The pattern was building up. She waited.

"People who know no better would easily believe that this man is one of East Germany's top-level spy masters, using his so-called anti-Fascist work as a cover.

"You see how it could appear. Herr Blake has been making inquiries about forged passports and identity papers. He has also displayed an unusual interest in cars crossing the border. We have evidence of this. One of those cars was driven by a certain taxi-driver who was later murdered. Herr Blake was in West Berlin at the time of the murder. And his only alibi, as I know, is yourself."

He touched his gloved fingers together and went on watching her and smiling.

"Prior to that, a certain undesirable character named Singer was murdered in Wedding. In his possession were some fifty mark notes—rather halves of fifty mark notes which had been torn. A typical method in the underworld of making sure against a double-cross."

He kept his glittering expressionless eyes on her. She felt she must be showing the fear that was growing in her.

After a pause he went on : "The other halves of those notes were in the possession of Herr Blake. Although he knew they were useless, he kept them. Human folly."

He looked quite sympathetic.

"Then there is the curious coincidence that Herr Blake was in Frankfurt am Main on the evening that another person of a most suspicious kind was murdered. Herr Blake was certainly in a public house near where this man was killed on that evening. The name was Grell and he was also knifed, like the taxi-driver."

Mary breathed deeply to still the fluttering in her stomach. So he meant to get at her through Steve. She had to betray either her father or Steve.

"Herr Blake is old enough to look after himself," she said.

Koll's expression let her understand that he could see through her bluff.

"That is not the point entirely, Fraulein Viner," he went on. "It is not only a question of the nature of Herr Blake's activities here—but also of your own.

"Let us suppose that military documents of a secret nature were found in Herr Blake's possession. Let us suppose too that your own fingerprints were found on the documents."

"You ought to be playing cowboys and Indians," Mary said. "Or should it be SS guards and Jews?"

His smile did not change.

"In a case which involved military espionage, it would be normal for it to be held *in camera*."

He spread his gloved hands palms up on the desk top.

Mary said: "You are forgetting that West Berlin is still an occupation zone with a British military presence."

"No. But the trial would take place in West Germany where, for the time being, we are more our own masters."

"That is all. I think you will see that from my point of view, this latter method has advantages in that it would perfectly ensure your silence. And since I would ensure that the documents would be concerned with British developments in nuclear weaponry, it should even raise German prestige in Whitehall.

"It is, however, complex and requires that several other persons would have to be taken into confidence.

"Therefore, on balance, I would sooner have you desist from your enquiries, sign a document as I said and leave it to the East Germans to make what bricks they can without straw. Take your time and think it over, Fraulein Viner."

She sat still, turning over all he had said. There was no doubt he could do it. The whole ghastly set-up was in their hands—police, secret service, army, courts. She was as powerless in West Berlin as though she were sitting in her father's old cell in Sachsenhausen. The old German imperial cadre had quietly and "democratically" resumed control. Through the Kaisers and the Prussian junker officer caste; through Hitler's Third Reich and the stormtroopers to the Christian Democrat Strauss and the neo-Nazis, the line ran unbroken.

Mary took out her cigarette packet and put a cigarette in her mouth with a hand that she could not quite prevent from shaking.

Fumbling in the bottom of her bag for her lighter, her hand touched the cold metal of Steve's revolver. She had forgotten it was there.

She lit the cigarette and sat with the lighter in her hand while a thrill of fearful exultation ran through her. She felt disembodied, at once excited and deadly calm.

She half finished her cigarette and threw it in the fire. Putting her lighter away, she gripped the butt of the revolver and curled her finger into the trigger guard. Steve had said that the safety catch had to be forward or back but she could not remember which.

Koll broke the silence.

"I have no wish to hurry you, Fraulein Viner, but I think it should not take long for you to see that there are only the ways I have suggested."

"No," she said. "There is another way."

He raised a polite eyebrow, waiting for her to explain.

"Suppose I were to kill you?"

He laughed.

"Fraulein Viner, you are not the only one who would like to do that. I really am well guarded."

"Not now," she said, and pulled the gun out. "Keep your hands flat on the desk."

His black-gloved hands twitched but stayed on the desk. She could see that every muscle of his shoulders was tensed. Narrow-eyed, he looked like a predator about to spring.

"Keep absolutely still," she said. He had not lost the advantage. She could not shoot a man in cold blood. Her brain raced, trying to recall what Steve had said about the safety catch. She sat with her thumb on the catch, facing Koll three yards away.

He was a trained man, she realized, and almost certainly had a weapon in his desk. He did not move but he was planning how to counter-attack.

Koll said quietly, in a friendly voice: "Let's stop bluffing. Shooting me, even if you could hit me, would do you no good."

He was trying to gain time, trying to distract her. Straining her nerves to stay alert, she did not take her eyes off Koll but within the fringe of her vision saw the revolver hammer rising. Koll saw it too and his hands tensed. She relaxed the trigger finger and was pleased to see sweat on his forehead.

Nor could he hide the deep exhalation he made as the hammer slowly returned to its position.

"It would be a police matter if I shot you," she said.

He smiled again.

"Oh, I know all about your Nazi police force here," Mary said. "But it would be a scandal. People would have to listen. How about your gas centrifuge agreement then, Herr Kessel? How about your fingerprints? They would become available, wouldn't they?"

All this talk. She should stop it. She was only giving away her indecision.

"And you would get twenty years," he countered.

"What! For killing an SS guard. I think not." She paused. "It is the only way."

Making a little gesture with his hands as though of surrender, he said: "I can see when I am beaten, Fraulein Viner. You may go. I shall give instructions for the release of Herr Blake."

"You must must think that I am a complete fool." Unless she did kill him she would never get out of his power. But still she knew she could not do it. He seemed to know it too.

He sat still, thinking. She twitched the gun and he pushed his hands further on the desk as though to emphasize his peaceful intentions.

He sighed and then said, very quietly: "There is one thing that you ought to know because it might make a difference to your attitude. Herr Viner was not in fact your father."

"Save your breath. I know that."

Although his expression did not change, the long pause showed that her answer surprised him.

"What you do not know, and what I do know, is who your actual father was."

"I don't want to hear," Mary shouted. "Be quiet. I warn you."

"I think you ought to know. It will interest you, especially since you are half a Jew. He was. . . ."

Mary raised her hands to cover her ears.

It was the moment Koll had worked for. In a flash he was up.

Mary brought the gun level and pulled the trigger.

It clicked harmlessly as he leapt round the desk, banging his thigh but recovering and coming on off balance.

Frantically she thumbed the safety catch forward and the gun fired as his hand reached it.

Through the ear-splitting din of the detonation she heard the thud as the pistol hit the wood panelling where his grab had flung it.

They stood facing each other, a foot apart. His hands clutched his right chest and his face was fixed in horrified surprise. Seconds passed and as blood seeped through his fingers, both looked down.

Mary instinctively made a gesture with her hand to help him but before she could do anything he sank to his knees with a long retching groan.

She watched him numbly as he crawled to the armchair, gasping. He managed to turn himself so that he was reclining against the side of the chair, his head in an ungainly position, one hand still pressing his chest above the liver. A pool of blood formed on the carpet under his elbow.

Somebody was hammering on the locked door and Dietrich was shouting : *"Was ist los? Mach auf!"*

It pulled Mary out of her daze and she went and fetched the pistol, from the corner where it had fallen.

Dietrich was hurling himself at the door.

Dietrich, organizer of all their failure—and worse.

The door started to spring and looked like giving.

"I shall shoot," she shouted, terrified that he might get in.

There was another shattering kick at the lock.

She pulled the trigger, hardly knowing that she had done so. A hole appeared, high up on the door.

It could not have hit him, but now there was silence.

Koll retched again. "God," he croaked in a low, strained voice, "She had a gun. Fools. Fools. Defeated by fools."

He looked up at Mary, still standing with the pistol held

gingerly in her hand. A bubbling croak came from his chest and blood trickled from his mouth.

"Doctor," he gasped.

Mary backed to the desk and felt for the phone with her left hand.

A car started up below and she looked out. The electronically operated gates slid aside and Dietrich drove out in the sports car, not looking back, tyres screeching with acceleration.

A ghastly bubbling came from Koll's throat, his eyes opened wide and lost their focus as he settled still lower. His blood-covered hand fell on the carpet. It was the first time Mary had seen a dead man.

She picked up the phone. It seemed to be a direct line to the switchboard of Koll Enterprises.

A girl's voice asked brightly: "*Bitte*, Herr Koll?"

"*Polizei, bitte,*" Mary answered.

PINNACLE BOOKS

THE INCREDIBLE ACTION PACKED SERIES

DEATH MERCHANT

by Joseph Rosenberger

His name is Richard Camellion, he's a master of disguise, deception and destruction. He does what the CIA and FBI cannot do. They call him THE DEATH MERCHANT!

Order		Title	Book #	Price
_____	# 1	THE DEATH MERCHANT	P0211	.95¢
_____	# 2	OPERATION OVERKILL	P245	.95¢
_____	# 3	THE PSYCHOTRAN PLOT	P117	.95¢
_____	# 4	CHINESE CONSPIRACY	P168	.95¢
_____	# 5	SATAN STRIKE	P182	.95¢
_____	# 6	ALBANIAN CONNECTION	P218	.95¢
_____	# 7	CASTRO FILE	P264	.95¢
_____	# 8	BILLIONAIRE MISSION	P339	.95¢

AND MORE TO COME . . .

TO ORDER

Please check the space next to the book/s you want, send this order form together with your check or money order, include the price of the book/s and 25¢ for handling and mailing to:

PINNACLE BOOKS, INC. / P.O. Box 4347
Grand Central Station / New York, N.Y. 10017

☐ CHECK HERE IF YOU WANT A FREE CATALOG

I have enclosed $_____ check_____ or money order_____
as payment in full. No C.O.D.'s

Name_____

Address_____

City_____ State_____ Zip_____
Please allow time for delivery)